Max stared at her, his face sad. "I followed you to Australia, Callie. But you'd already left Sydney by the time I got there, and I couldn't track you after that."

"You followed me?" Shock held her immobile for several seconds. "Why?" she finally demanded.

"Because there are things I need to know, stuff we have to talk about." His lips tightened to a thin, angry line at the shake of her head. "What?"

"I don't want to talk about the past ever again." She turned a

"Well, I do. I d you're going know everything, then and only then off with those divorce papers you're so anxious to file."

Despite the blazing September sun and the protection of the cabin, Callie felt an icy breeze across her nerves.

Max could never know the truth. Never.

Books by Lois Richer

Love Inspired Suspense

Love Inspired

LOIS RICHER

Sneaking a flashlight under the blankets, hiding in a thicket of Caragana bushes where no one could see, pushing books into socks to take to camp—those are just some of the things Lois Richer freely admits to in her pursuit of the written word. "I'm a bookaholic. I can't do without stories," she confesses. "It's always been that way."

Lois Richer

IDENTITY: UNDERCOVER

Steeple Hill®

Published by Steeple Hill Books™

STEEPLE HILL BOOKS

Steeple Hill®

ISBN-13: 978-0-373-87395-1
ISBN-10:   0-373-87395-6

IDENTITY: UNDERCOVER

Copyright © 2006 by Lois M. Richer

www.SteepleHill.com

Printed in U.S.A.

You have seen me tossing and turning through the night. You have collected all my tears and preserved them in a bottle! You have recorded every one in your book...This one thing I know: God is for me!
—*Psalms* 56:8, 9b

This book is gratefully dedicated to those who keep our countries safe, who stand at the entrance of freedom and say, "I will lay down my life to preserve you." May we never fail them.

PROLOGUE

This above all—to thine own self be true.
                    —William Shakespeare

Ten years ago

The courtroom brimmed with reporters, all present to record every sordid detail they could glean about the ambassador's daughter and her sad little tale.

Callie Merton took a deep breath, forced herself to walk calmly to the front of the room. Marie Antoinette going to the guillotine, that's who she'd pretend to be.

She took the oath, sat down, faced straight ahead. Using every morsel of control she could scrounge, she answered the questions clearly and concisely, remembering the prosecutor's advice to keep it short and simple.

"The man who gave you the drugs—do you see him in the courtroom today?"

"Yes."

"Would you point to that person?"

She lifted her hand, aimed one finger. "That's him."

A rumble of whispers rippled through the audience.

"Let the record show that the witness has identified the defendant."

There were more questions. Lots of them. Horrible, probing questions that left no tawdry point hidden. Clinging to her icy mantle of aloofness, Callie refused to be swayed.

At last she was released. Holding her head high, she stepped down, toward the man she'd accused. Every nerve in her body pulled taut in tense anticipation as she neared the place where he sat, the place she had to pass to get out of this room, away from the prying eyes.

She'd almost passed him when his voice, whisper-soft but brimming with menace, reached her.

"You'll pay for this. No matter how long it takes, you'll pay."

Callie kept walking, down the long aisle, past the photographers with their whirring cameras, out of the building. Fifteen granite steps got her to the street level. From there it was a short dash to her car. Only when she was inside with the doors locked did she fill her lungs with a deep breath.

Then Callie drove as far and as fast as she dared. When she finally stopped running, she was on a ferry that would take her to the city of Victoria, British Columbia.

By then she'd left Marie Antoinette far behind, had turned into someone else, a gutsy young woman who didn't live in fear but took on the next phase of her life with dignity and pride. One who accepted challenges as a way to prove she'd changed.

But that woman was a charade.

And every so often a voice from the past would whisper through her head reminding her that the real Callie Merton had gone undercover.

ONE

Present Day

"We have a mission for you, Callie."

The owner of Finders Inc. had a reputation for directness. Callie met Shelby Kincaid-Austen's scrutiny head-on and forced herself not to flinch at the flicker of compassion she glimpsed in the other woman's eyes.

"Great. I was hoping you'd have something for me." Since Shelby didn't ask about the time she'd taken off, Callie allowed herself to relax just a little.

"I'm assuming you have no preference about location?"

"As long as it's not Australia again. I'm really tired of the Outback, mate."

"I'm sorry that one took so long." Shelby nodded, but her face remained neutral. "I only agreed to assign it to you because you said you needed something that would keep you out of the country for a while."

Callie noted Shelby's pause, meant to allow her the opportunity to discuss what had happened to cause that request. Callie remained silent, unmoving. After a moment Shelby shrugged, continued.

"You're one of the best locators we have so this assignment shouldn't be too difficult."

"None of them start out that way." Callie leaned forward. "What should I know?"

"Finders Inc. has been hired to locate a man named Josiah Harpnell as quickly as we can. He's the recipient of a substantial legacy. There are certain papers that require his signature—legal technicalities but necessary nonetheless. Though several messages have been forwarded to Mr. Harpnell's last known address, he has not responded to any of them."

"Messages—so you didn't talk to him? I'm guessing that means he has no access to a phone. Any idea where he is now?"

"Alaska."

"Well, that's pinpointing it." Callie grimaced. "From the front burner of the Outback to the freezer of Alaska. What more could a girl want?"

Quite a lot, actually. But since it was highly unlikely she'd ever get back the one thing she longed for, Callie focused on business and Shelby.

"I know it's not much to go on. It's a big area and our Intel is sketchy at best."

"I'm listening."

Shelby leaned her elbows on her desk, tented her fingers.

"From what we understand, Mr. Harpnell lives in the wilds, off the land—by choice. The last mailing address we had for him is in Ketchikan but his current physical location isn't certain and you may need to change destinations along the way. If you can be ready in two days, I'll arrange passage for you. A friend of mine is cruising up the coast and has agreed to take you."

"Sail?" That was new.

"I'll explain in a minute but let me say now that your journey north will give us time to update our information. Tomorrow you can visit the estate, learn exactly what's at stake."

Late September hardly seemed the time to sail north, though Callie suddenly remembered Max had once said sailing the Inside Passage in the fall was—

Like a shutter she clicked those thoughts out of her mind.

"What else?"

"I can't tell you much more until research has finished their part. Once you're in Ketchikan, you'll be in a better position to decide the next step for yourself. The important thing is to find this man and get his signature on the documents."

It sounded fairly straightforward. Callie nodded. "Okay, I'll do it."

"You may need some kind of cover story. I'd thought perhaps you could start out as if you're a tourist, maybe an Aussie backpacker. You've picked up the accent like a native, better than anyone I've ever seen, so you should be able to ask a lot of questions about the area without being suspect."

"If this Harpnell fellow isn't there, you want me to keep following the trail, right?"

"It's urgent that we locate him, Callie, and soon. If something should happen to him before the papers are signed, since he has no legal heir, the government will take over his estate. A lot of historical artifacts in that house will be sold off for a pittance."

"Okay."

Shelby stared at the file in her hand, then lifted her gaze to center on Callie.

"Understand that Harpnell doesn't have to come back. Once the paperwork is in place, he can assign someone to look after things or dispose of them as he wishes. Apparently that's what his half brother intended. He's the one who left him the place and everything in it."

"Is there a Mrs. Harpnell?"

"Josiah was married briefly many years ago but they divorced a year later. She had a child from an earlier marriage but Josiah never adopted him so the child has no legal standing with the courts as far as we know."

"Okay." Callie rose, grabbed her bag and headed for the door. "I'll get down to the briefing room and take a look at the file. The estate info is in it?"

"All the details we have are there. There's just one more thing." Shelby's voice brimmed with warning. "We have reason to believe that someone else knows about this inheritance and that they will make an attempt to somehow acquire it. You could experience some danger. Briefing will relate the problems two other agencies have experienced so far, but I'll tell you this, there have been several unusual occurrences."

Callie understood what she meant. Someone was trying to upset the apple cart. Money did that to people.

"That's why you want your friend to get me up there via sailboat, I'm assuming."

"Yes." Shelby nodded, her expression serious. "Ordinarily we'd attempt to get his signature by mail, but that's already been tried—and failed. Miserably. These problems are the reason we need you to hand carry the necessary documents and bring them back. As a notary you're licensed to witness Mr. Harpnell's signature, which will satisfy the legal requirements. That's another reason why I chose you."

"Okay."

"We want those documents back here as soon as possible so we can file them with the court, Callie."

"Why the rush?" she mused aloud. "There's no time limit is there?"

Daniel McCullough, CEO of Finders Inc., shoved open Shelby's door and stepped into the room, his smile huge.

"About time you got back to this country, kiddo." He wrapped Callie in a bear hug, then tapped the end of her nose before grinning at Shelby. "I heard the last question—let me answer." He turned back to Callie.

"Before the case was brought to our attention, the lawyers tried several other locators—with no success. In fact, several people were hurt in the process. They came to us because of our reputation for completing every case, and because time is running out. We must have the papers signed within two weeks, or the government becomes the administrator of the estate to dispose of at its discretion."

"And you don't think they're up to it or what?" The inflection in Daniel's voice told Callie the story was not complete.

"Let us just say we've learned that the person who would be handling this estate as the government's representative has been approached to disperse the historical and very rare artifacts to purchasers who have no interest in preserving our country's heritage."

"Not only would that be a great loss," Shelby added, "but it goes against everything the owner of the estate wanted, and that's not even mentioning that the money would be wasted. The estate is quite large as you'll see when you visit it. Management fees would eat it up."

"Okay, then. Good to know." Callie turned to leave. "I'll get to work on Josiah's background."

"In a minute."

The worry threading through Shelby's voice drew her attention. She faced the other woman, schooling her features to conceal any emotion. She was good at that.

"I'm worried about you, Callie. You're so thin and pale. You're sure you want to do this?"

"I'm sure. And I'm fine. See you." Callie walked out of Shelby's office and found Daniel had followed her. He matched his step to hers.

"I wouldn't say you look good, Callie, but you look better than the last time you were in."

"So do you." She tilted her head, winked. "Three months of marriage must agree with you. I hear Samantha turned down a promotion. She's got to be really happy being your wife to willingly give up her dream job."

"I hope she's happy." Daniel's cheeks darkened in embarrassment. "But turning down that promotion was totally her choice. I won't say I'm not glad, though. We never expected to start a family so soon after we married—we especially didn't expect to parent twins— but we're both glad about it."

"Twins?" Callie grinned, delighted that the couple had been so blessed, though a little hidden nerve in her heart renewed its persistent throb.

"Sam says she's had enough fieldwork for a while. She comes into the office to help with training but that will probably end in a few months. She's already finding the pregnancy very tiring." He paused, stopped Callie from entering the elevator by placing his hand on her wrist. His eyes darkened, grew sad. "I'm sorry if I'm hurting you by telling you this, Callie."

"Of course you're not hurting me. I'm happy for you both." She smiled to show she meant it, shielding the ache she was afraid would never go away.

"Thank you." But the question remained in his eyes.

"Look, Daniel, things happen, change. That's the way life is. I really am happy for both of you." She met his stare and held it, knowing he'd see beyond her mask if she let him. "Bad things happened, but I have to get on with living. This case will give me the perfect opportunity to start over."

"I guess. If that's what you want." His amber eyes peered through the black-rimmed glasses, a reprimand lurking in their depths. "You do know Max has contacted me. Several times. I told him what you said, but I felt like a heel doing it." He touched her arm. "You have to talk to him yourself, Callie."

"We did talk. Too much." She shook her head. "I don't have anything to say that Max Chambers wants to hear. Anyway, it's too late for talking. The past is over, finished."

"Who are you trying to convince, sweetie? Me, or you?" Daniel bent, brushed her cheek with a brotherly kiss. "Don't be so hard on yourself. Keep depending on God. He'll work it out."

"Yeah." Like God had done so much for her already.

Callie reached up and hugged him. "That's for you to pass on to Sam. Tell her—tell her to take care. And that I love her."

"I will." He stood watching as she stepped into the elevator, a frown disturbing his handsome features.

Well, why wouldn't he frown? He and Max had been good friends. And she'd come between them.

Memories of that painful era threatened to burst through Callie's fragile defenses and explode her thinly held self-control. Her defenses weren't quite as strong as she wanted. Yet.

Determined no one would see her weaken, she stepped out of the elevator and slipped into a nearby ladies' room where she splashed cold water on her face until she'd regained her composure. Once she was centered and in control again she made her way to the briefing room.

After absorbing a minutiae of details about Josiah Harpnell, Callie glanced up from her file, found Daniel lounging in the doorway, watching her.

"Well?"

"About what I expected. The estate is massive. Less detail on Josiah than usual, but then this case is different for Finders Inc., isn't it?"

"Every case is different, but we usually have more to go on than what we've been able to give you." He sank down onto a stool opposite her. "Callie, I have to tell Max something. He's just called again, desperate to get in touch with you."

And she knew exactly why.

"Maybe you don't believe me but he's out of his mind with worry, Callie. He cares about you."

She couldn't say anything, simply sat staring at her hands, waiting.

"He's my friend, honey. Max is the closest thing I've had to a brother since Grant died." His voice begged her to reconsider. "I can't be your go-between anymore. I've got to tell him the truth. The two of you need to talk this out."

Daniel didn't know it but there was nothing for them to talk about. He wouldn't understand that Max was only trying to do the right thing, to adhere to those principles he clung to so strongly. Daniel wouldn't understand that she couldn't bear to go back, to look into those eyes and see what lay there—the condemnation he never spoke of.

"Please, Callie. Just see him, let him know you're all right."

It was unavoidable and she knew it. The one last thing she had to do before the past was finally over, irrevocably finished.

"When do I ship out?" she whispered.

"Day after tomorrow, 7:00 a.m."

"Fine. I'll check out Josiah Harpnell's estate tomorrow. You tell Max I'll meet him at the Harbor Café at six-thirty the following morning."

"I'll tell him right away." Daniel's face beamed. "Thank you, Callie. I promise you won't regret it." He rose, turned to leave.

"There's just one catch."

Daniel froze, twisted to stare at her, a frown marring his thin face.

"After that it's over. No more phone calls, no more contacting you about me, nothing."

Daniel opened his mouth to protest but Callie held up a hand.

"I appreciate all you've tried to do, Daniel, but my marriage to Max is over. Those are my terms. If he's there, I'll know he accepts them. If he's not, fine. The choice is up to him."

While Daniel was still speechless, she gathered up her things, shoved them into her backpack and left the room, the building, to return to the small bleak square that now served as home base.

It was a good thing Shelby had assigned this mission. Otherwise Callie knew there would be little point to the rest of her life.

Someone was watching her.

Callie could feel the burn right through her windbreaker to the back of her neck. But no matter how closely she scrutinized the area, it was impossible to see exactly who it was.

The same thing had happened the day before when she'd visited the estate Josiah would inherit. Whoever it was knew how to keep a low profile.

Truthfully, she'd expected someone to take an interest in her appearance there. Finders already knew someone didn't want Josiah gaining control of the estate. What they didn't know was why.

But she'd find out. She always did. And maybe in the meantime she'd discover why they had followed her.

Callie glanced at her watch for the thousandth time and finally admitted what her brain didn't want to accept.

Max wasn't coming.

The knowledge burned a hole straight to her heart,

but she ignored the pain, paid for her coffee and left the restaurant. As she rounded the corner and moved toward the craft that would transport her to Ketchikan, she had to sidestep a crowd.

Callie wove her way among the group of curious bystanders and fought to get a better look through the throng of shoulders and heads. What she saw made her gasp: four trim, elegant offshore cruisers still tied to the dock lay listing to the west, badly damaged and taking on water faster than it could be bailed out.

"What happened?" she asked the person beside her.

"Problems with the ferry," he said. "Should never have come near those boats. Must have been something mechanical that made it veer so close. The captain did some very snappy maneuvering to get it docked but not before it scraped those four beauties. The repair bills are going to be astronomical."

He was right. Even from this distance she could see that repairs to *The Marguerite*, her ride, were going to take a lot longer than a few hours. Farther down the dock one of the B.C. ferries lay battered and bruised, but securely tied in place.

Callie pulled out her cell phone to tell Shelby she was going to take the ferry to Ketchikan, but paused in the middle of dialing as she caught a fragment of the conversation nearby.

"The ferry's out of service till the investigation's complete," she heard someone behind her grumble. "They say they can't get a replacement here till late tonight."

Callie snapped her phone closed, walked away from the mess as she tried to figure out her next move.

"Callie?"

It wasn't the hand on her arm that made her freeze, it was the voice. Totally devoid of all the assurance Max Chambers's firm tones had once boasted, his low utterance now sounded hesitant, unsure, as if he was afraid to talk to her. She turned, faced him, and wondered if it had been *his* eyes she'd felt watching her.

"You're late."

It wasn't the best thing she could have said, but Callie was furious that he'd shown up now, after she'd shoved away hope and the past and begun to concentrate on her job.

"I'm sorry. There's road construction everywhere. I got caught in a detour. I couldn't help it." His eyes—shimmers of dark green with flecks of seafoam, held hers for just an instant before he took in the scene. "What happened here?"

"A ferry hit some boats." She moved her arm so his hand fell away. "I can't talk to you now, Max. I'm on assignment. I've got to get up north." She turned away, checked with operations at Finders, learned that flights into Ketchikan were sold out. Now what?

"Wherever you're going, Callie, I'll take you."

"I'm sure you've got to go to work."

"Nope." He shook his head, his smile faintly mocking. "I sold the business, remember?"

"You sold Chambers and Son?" She could hardly believe it. "But it was the family business. It was your dream."

He shook his head. "It was never mine. For a while I thought it was my job to keep the family business going but eventually Dad convinced me I needed to live my own dream."

"Doing what?"

"Designing boats." He grinned at her. "In a way I was already doing that, suggesting alterations and special orders for the clients. Now I plan it all into the original design. My design. Somebody else builds them."

"Oh. I didn't know." This was a side of him she'd never seen. He looked at peace about his decision, relaxed, but in a different way than he'd looked at the publicity launches of his company's sailboats. "I—I've been away."

"I know. I've tried to reach you a hundred times to talk to you." His face tightened. "I didn't expect that when you finally contacted me it would be with divorce papers."

Trust Max to get to the root of the problem without wasting time.

"We both know it's over. Why prolong things? I spent a lot of time thinking about us on my last assignment." She faced him, chin thrust out, shoulders back. "I'm not what you need or want, Max. I never liked posing for the cameras, being your photo-op partner. I ruin things, spoil your image. You yourself said I was bad for business."

He winced at the reminder.

"I was mad. That hull cost—no!" He bit his lip, shook his head. "No. I'm not doing this again, Callie. I promised myself that when I finally got to talk to you it would not be about the past. Whatever was, was. We can't change it. I'm more interested in the future."

"We don't have a future. That's *why* I had those papers sent." She glanced at her watch, grimaced. "This isn't the place nor the time. I've got to find some way to get out of here."

"I told you, I'll take you." He pushed his hands into

the pockets of his perfectly pressed khaki pants. His white shirt lay open at the throat, displaying his tanned neck. Max was always tanned. He wore his navy jacket half-zipped in that usual carelessly elegant way that suited him so well. The hesitancy she'd thought she'd glimpsed at first was gone now. Everything about him screamed self-assured confidence.

Beside him Callie felt as she always had—underdressed, out of place, a mess. "You don't know where I'm going," she blurted out.

"Somewhere north," he guessed. "I always sail north in the fall. You know that. I'll drop you wherever you need to be."

She said nothing, silently calculating her options—which took about two seconds.

"I'll have to okay it with Daniel," she told him.

Maybe she could ask for a replacement while she was at it, because she did not, under any circumstances, want to be stuck for hours on end, on a sailboat with Max Chambers—even one as deluxe as his *Freedom*. It was too dangerous.

"Finders doesn't like exceptions to the rules. Daniel may not go for it."

"I think he'll approve of this."

Implying that Max was the exception to Daniel's rules. Hadn't he always been?

"Go ahead. I'll wait."

Callie dialed, explained the situation, then cut short Daniel's expressions of delight that she and Max would have time to talk on the voyage north.

"I'm just accepting passage," she told him in a whisper. "There's nothing more to it." She clicked the phone closed.

If Max heard her, he gave no sign, simply stood waiting, watching.

"I supposed *Freedom*'s berthed in the usual place?" she asked, wishing they didn't have to waste time driving to his marina.

"*Freedom*'s in dry dock. Repairs," he said, answering her question before she could ask it. He pointed to a slip several hundred feet in the opposite direction. "That's *Hope*. She's fully loaded and ready for passage, if you are. I moor her here because it's nearer the condo."

That condo—it had been at the core of many of their disputes. Callie wanted to ask him what had happened to the house—the beautiful house she'd once called home, but she didn't dare. The memories were too raw.

"Is there anything you need to do before we leave?" Max asked politely as they walked toward the sparkling white craft.

"No. I'm ready to go." She followed him to the boat, waited while he boarded, then handed over her backpack before stepping onto the glossy deck.

"Welcome aboard."

"She's very beautiful, Max," she murmured, taking in the highly polished wood, the lazy loungers, a table and chairs at the bow where two could share dinner under the stars. "When did you get her?"

"She was finished a month ago." He began preparations for casting off. "Entirely my design."

Callie had sailed with him enough to know the procedures but she'd never been any good at figuring out what he wanted her to do next so she sat at the front and waited for instructions.

None came. He probably figured she'd mess up or

worse, ruin his perfect creation. That's what Max loved most—perfection. It was also what she'd never been able to achieve.

While she sat remembering past days she'd spent sailing with him, the boat slipped from its berth and moved out of the harbor. The motor picked up speed as they began gliding over the water, following the coastline in an in-and-out pattern that Callie didn't understand. But she had full confidence in Max. He'd grown up exploring these waters and even though the sails on this boat remained tied down, she knew he'd be gauging the wind, the current, the tides, choosing the perfect path to get them on their way.

Suddenly she realized that she hadn't told him their destination. Callie rose, gingerly made her way up to the captain's deck where Max stood, the wind dragging the walnut-colored strands of his hair off his face. His joy in the day was apparent.

"We're heading for Ketchikan," she told him.

"I know. Daniel told me."

She couldn't believe it.

"I forced it out of him when I talked to him yesterday," Max admitted. "I couldn't take not knowing anymore."

"Why should you know?" Anger, icy and hot at the same time, rolled through her. "This is *my* job. I don't know everything about your life."

"You could. I'd gladly tell you anything you want to know if you'd ever ask." He stared at her, his face sad. "I followed you to Australia, Callie. But you'd already left Sydney by the time I got there and I couldn't track you after that."

"You followed me?" Shock held her immobile for several seconds. "Why?" she finally demanded.

"Because there are things I need to know, stuff we have to talk about." His lips tightened to a thin, angry line at the shake of her head. "What?"

"I don't want to talk about the past, Max. Not ever again." She turned away but his words stopped her.

"Well I do. And for as long as I've got you on my boat, we're going to talk about it. I need to know the truth, Callie. And you're going to tell it to me. When I'm satisfied I know everything, then and only then will I send you off with those divorce papers you're so anxious to file."

Despite the blazing September sun and the protection of the cabin, an icy-cold breeze tap-danced over Callie's nerves.

Max couldn't know the truth.

Not ever.

TWO

Max pushed his sunglasses onto the top of his head and stared at the coastline as his forefinger massaged his temple.

"Callie? Can you come here for a minute? Please?"

He wouldn't blame her if she ignored him completely. He'd been a total jerk to act as he had, to make her feel as if he'd deliberately cornered her onboard to force her to explain.

Though it wasn't an excuse, the way he'd been served those papers—the fact that he had been served them at all, made him see red. When she refused to talk to him he'd completely lost all perspective.

Callie responded, but not quickly. He watched her carefully store away the papers she'd been studying. She tucked them into her backpack and stowed it under the seat before she moved toward him.

Max realized how badly he'd fooled himself into believing that all Callie needed was time, that eventually she'd come home and they could start over. He'd never imagined, never let himself even consider that what she really wanted was to escape him.

"You bellowed?" Callie stood poised on the top step,

curls dancing in the wind, eyes shadowed by the dark glasses she wore.

"Sorry. I just wanted to tell you that I've got to take a break. I've got a killer headache." He pointed ahead. "There's a little cove there that we can pull into. Is that okay with you?"

"I guess." She pulled her glasses off to study him. Her blue eyes darkened with uncertainty. "Do you want me to take the wheel?"

"No." A surge of frustration bubbled inside his heart when she glanced at her watch then frowned. The words burst out before he could check them. "Don't worry. I won't hold up your mission. I just need a break."

"Fine. We'll take a break. Do you want something to drink?"

"Coffee would be nice." *And some tape on my mouth to hold it shut so I won't say anything else stupid.*

"Fine. Coffee it is." She turned, walked down the steps. A few minutes later he heard the rattle of the coffee pot. Every so often the rich aroma of percolating grounds caught on the breeze and filled his nostrils, hailing reminders of other sailing days when life with Callie had seemed good, right. Forever.

Long ago days.

Max edged his way into the bay, dropped anchor and climbed down from his perch. Callie had an umbrella set up over one of the loungers. Two steaming cups sat on the side table, one of them filled with a rich mocha-colored liquid.

Strong and creamy. At least she remembered that much.

"Thank you," he murmured, sinking into the chaise. He took a sip of the smooth, creamed coffee, then let his head tip back against the chair as the pounding took over. He pretended he couldn't feel her watching him.

"I suppose I should be able to take over the helm but I'll be just as happy if I don't have to. I guess that doesn't make me a very good sailing partner." The words died away.

After a moment she spoke again, her voice brimming with hesitancy and something else—shame?

"But then I never was a very good partner, period."

He hated her saying that, hated that he'd obviously made her so unhappy.

"Callie?" Max reached out, grasped her wrist before she could move away. Though he could tell she didn't like his grip, she remained still. "Could we please just let the past lie for a while? You don't want to talk about what happened between us. Fine. I'll try to abide by that. But could we at least make an attempt to enjoy this trip?"

"While I'm a prisoner, you mean?" She did slide her hand away then. Her jaw thrust forward in defiance, letting him know she wouldn't forgive him so easily.

"Come on, Cal," Max chided, almost smiling at her stubborn tip-tilted chin. "You're not a prisoner and you know it. Anytime you ask, I'll drop you off at the nearest town."

"That's not what you said."

"I know." He took another sip and decided it was long past time for the truth. "Those papers made me mad, Callie and I reacted badly. We don't see each other for ages, I can't get hold of you, don't know whether you're alive or dead, and suddenly some man I've never even seen before serves me with divorce papers in front of a crowd of people I'm trying to persuade to buy one of my designs."

"So I embarrassed you with my bad timing. Again." She winced. "I didn't know. I'm sorry."

"It wasn't the timing, Callie."

"Whatever it was, then. I'm still sorry. I'm always sorry. But it doesn't seem to help much." She flopped down opposite him, sipped her own coffee.

Max shook his head, sought for the right words.

"After the ba—when you left, you said you were taking another job because you had to get away, to think things over. Then you wrote you needed more time to get past…"

He swallowed hard, tiptoed around that subject.

"I agreed because I figured some space might be good for both of us. But I've hardly heard from you, I never know where you are. You certainly never once said anything about divorce in those cryptic little notes Finders Inc. forwarded to me."

"Again—I'm sorry," she whispered but she didn't look at him.

Max was heartily sick of hearing that word, but at the moment there seemed little else either of them could say. He was sorry, too. He'd made his own mistakes, pushed when he should have just been there for her.

As he studied her, Max suddenly realized that this woman was not the Callie Merton he'd married. Body and mind were there. But her soul, the essence that made Callie who she was, now hid in a mask of protection that prevented him from reading her real emotions. She seemed as confident as always, but was it real or simply a front—something to keep him from getting too close?

Callie lifted her cup and he noticed her hand was shaking. He took a second, more deliberate survey of his wife, sans sunglasses and hat. The sight stunned him. There were dark rings around her eyes, she was far too thin, her cheekbones too pronounced even for a fashion model. Physically she looked like she was at the end of her rope. That wouldn't affect her job, of course. She still projected the same confidence she'd always had in her work. The cause of her frailty must lie elsewhere. It had stolen the joy from her eyes.

Daniel's warning that Callie had changed rang true. The more Max studied her, the more he realized that she was forcing herself to sit here, to talk to him. She seemed un-usually nervous about it and he couldn't help wondering if maybe seeing him again had helped twig old memories for her, too. Maybe she was rethinking the divorce.

Maybe he still had a chance.

Until now he'd thought only of his own hurt, anger, disappointment. He'd seen himself as the wronged party. But it was clear Callie wasn't at peace despite her decision to cut herself off from him.

"Can you tell me anything about this mission?" Maybe the reason God had brought them together was for him to help her somehow. "What's supposed to happen when you get to Ketchikan?"

In the past Max had helped out Finders Inc. several times and as a result Daniel had granted him a certain security clearance. Surely Callie remembered that and wouldn't try to block his questions, because if she did he'd phone Daniel and get the truth. And while Max had the CEO on the phone, he'd ask him a few hard ques-tions about her latest physical.

"I have to find a man, get him to sign some papers. Piece of cake."

"Can I know the name of the man?"

She looked at him, raised one eyebrow. "Why?"

"Just curious."

She lay back on the lounger, kicked off her deck shoes and stretched her toes in the sun. "Josiah Harpnell. Ring any bells for you?"

Max nodded. "As a matter of fact it does. He published some research on the grazing paths of caribou and elk herds when they migrate north in the summer. Once the environmentalists got hold of it in Washington, there were fireworks. I think that was about two years ago."

"You were considering entering politics then."

She said it with a certain resignation that made Max remember how much she'd hated his constant political glad-handing, the unending meetings, phone calls, game playing. It was one reason she gave for continuing her killer schedule at Finders Inc. One of many reasons. It was also the argument she'd used against starting the family he thought they'd both wanted.

"I was on a committee to investigate some of Harpnell's claims," he mused, dredging up the information. "There was concern that the old migration routes would be disturbed by plans to dig for oil in a protected area." To ease the throbbing at the back of his neck, Max attempted to massage away the pain. "I'm glad I realized that political life wasn't for me."

"To give you more time to focus on your business interests, you said."

That had been the reason he'd given her, but even back then, Max had known something was wrong between them, that Callie was using his political leanings as an excuse to stay busy and away from him. He'd assumed that cutting back on his schedule would fix whatever wasn't working with them. He'd been wrong.

"This spring I resigned from a lot of the committees I'm on," he explained. "Chamber of Commerce, City Council, all of it. Except for the church. I'm still a member there."

"Ah, yes. The church." Her voice brimmed with scathing and he recalled how uncomfortable she'd always seemed in the church he'd attended since he was a child.

"My church is important to me."

"I know." She watched him through narrowed eyes.

Max leaned back, tried not to wince at the increased pounding. Now of all times he didn't want to look weak—but Callie already knew about his killer headaches. Her narrowed scrutiny wouldn't miss a thing. He closed his eyes, feigned sleep.

"Look at me, Max." She grasped his chin, forced him to look at her. "Is it a migraine? Because you don't have to go with me you know. I can manage on my own. I always do."

As if she hadn't told him that a thousand times before. "It's just a headache."

"You're sure?" Callie's fingers dropped from his face, wrapped around his wrist.

She was taking his pulse, he realized suddenly. The feel of her skin brought back a thousand memories… He yanked his hand away.

"I don't need your first aid, Callie. I know Finders equips you to handle anything, but I'm fine. I'll rest for a bit and it will go away."

"That's what you always said—right before it turned into a whopper." She leaned closer to check his pupils.

Max caught the lemony scent of her favorite shampoo and shifted away from temptation. Callie glared at him.

"Why didn't you mention you had a headache? You can hardly expect it to go away while you're squinting into the sun." Her voice lowered, sounded almost friendly. "I've got some medication. Do you want a tablet?"

"Sure." Anything to ease the band of pain that was making his eyes blur and weakening his ability to remain angry at her.

A few moments later he swallowed the medication she offered then forced himself to lie prone on the lounger as the gentle lap of the waves lulled him into a dreamy floating state. It reminded him of the second honeymoon he'd thought about surprising her with many times in the past. Somehow he'd never gotten around to planning it. What had he been doing that was so important?

"I could man the helm for a while if you want," Callie offered after a long silence.

"Thanks anyway, but I'd like to keep this boat in its present condition."

Max bit his tongue, opened one eye to see how she'd taken his rude and unnecessary rebuff.

"Yeah, sure. I guess sailing was like a lot of other things in our marriage. I never did get the hang of it," she mumbled, her face bright red.

He ignored the last part, tried to make a joke of her ineptness at steering a craft.

"Your problem with direction while sailing is rather strange when you consider the job you do, isn't it?" Whatever she'd given him was working fast. Max felt the bolts of pain that gripped his brain loosening. His whole body was relaxing inch by inch. "Daniel said you're one of the best locators Finders has."

"Daniel's a very nice man."

"Daniel doesn't exaggerate." He stared at her and wished Callie would open up and just talk, let the words flow without checking every sentence, without censoring every word. Once he'd thought it was shyness, thought she'd get over it. He knew better than that now. Callie kept a tight rein on herself all the time, but now the rein was choking her. "How can you locate a thing or a person if you don't know your directions?"

"I don't get my directions confused on land, Maxwell. Just when I'm on the water, when I don't have any reference points. On good old terra firma I know exactly where I'm going. It's a land sense, I guess. Something I was born with. As opposed to sea sense."

Better. At least she was talking.

"What were you doing in Australia?"

"Locating a creep." She made a face. "Worst assignment I ever had."

"Why?" Immediately his radar went up.

"Nothing horrible. It was just busywork once I located him, tailing him to make sure he didn't disappear." She gave him a sideways look while considering her answer. "The guy was a total sleazebag. He made his second home in the bars, nightclubs, strip joints— all the garbage Sydney and every other city has to offer."

Callie had never really told him much about her work before. He'd told himself it was a security thing, or because she wanted their time together to be free of Finders Inc., but his heart had known better. Max felt a wiggle of satisfaction that she'd willingly explained this much with so little prodding.

"How long did you follow him?"

"Two months, day and night."

"And in all that time he didn't notice you?" He could hardly believe it.

Even thin as a rail, Callie was gorgeous. A cap of curls that shone like rubbed mahogany, sapphire-blue eyes and a mouth that tilted upward in an impish grin when she laughed. She was tall and slim with a swift agility he'd always admired. How could anyone not notice Callie Merton?

"We use disguises, Max." She made a face. "Trust me, he never even knew I was there."

"Why were you tailing him for so long?" he asked, curious as to whether her absence from his world all that time had been by choice or by request. "You used to take cases that lasted only a week or two."

"Our client didn't want him to go missing before they could get immigration to bring him back into the country and since I was already on the case—" She shrugged. "It wasn't as bad as I made it out to be. He usually slept till noon or later. Believe me, I got lots of time on the beach. The ocean was great and I soaked up a few rays, as well."

She didn't look tanned and rested. She looked—tense.

Callie wasn't telling him everything. Max had a hunch it was important to find out what she'd deliberately omitted. In the past he'd shied away from asking too many questions. Maybe that had been a mistake.

"He stole some crack from a fellow who doesn't like to be messed with. To get away, our boy headed for the

Outback." She grimaced. "There my cover was that I was a scientist conducting experiments in the area. Once he dried out, we got to be pals. There were no bars in the area, you see. When immigration finally picked him up, I think he'd been sober the longest in his life."

"Some good from the bad then." He kept his focus on her, realized she wasn't going to tell him any more.

"I suppose, though it took me a couple of hours in the shower to get rid of all that dust. It's not a place I'd recommend as a holiday spot even though it is beautiful." Callie grinned at him, blue eyes dancing with fun. "It sure cured me of camping, though. I don't think I ever want to sleep in a tent again."

"That's something to be thankful for." He grinned back, remembering the first few months they'd been married. How many weekends had he left work early, packed up their sleeping bags and that ratty tent she loved? He'd trekked behind her up and down the mountain for miles until she found exactly the right place to make camp so they could sleep in the outdoors.

"I think I'm too old to sleep on the ground again."

"Me, too." She giggled.

The laughter died away until only silence hung between them.

"I'm sorry that I hurt you, Max," she whispered, her voice so faint he had to lean in to hear. "I didn't mean to do that. It's just—I can't stay married to you anymore."

"Why?" He needed something to silence the desperate whisper in his heart. What they'd shared couldn't be beyond repair. He wouldn't accept that. "What was it I did that was so terrible you had to run away, and keep running?"

"It wasn't you!" She stared at him, her eyes huge in her heart-shaped face. "Of course it wasn't you. It was me. It *is* me. I'm an embarrassment to you, a nuisance, the proverbial square peg in a round hole."

"Callie, that's not true."

"Of course it is." She shook her head, her face rueful. "Did you think I didn't notice how many times you had to apologize for me to your friends, your employees, your family?"

"I didn't apologize for you!" She made it sound like he'd been ashamed of her. That had never been true.

"You did, Max." She nodded her head, curls tumbling down over one eye. She shoved them out of the way. "That time I tried to bring a casserole to the church pot-luck—don't you remember? 'Callie didn't realize,' you told them."

"Well you didn't, but that was my fault for not explaining that it was supposed to be a dessert potluck." He couldn't fathom the cause of the despair flooding her face. "What was wrong with saying that?"

"Nothing. Except that you had to keep saying it. Over and over. 'Excuse Callie.' 'Sorry, Callie didn't understand.' 'Poor dumb Callie.'" She laughed but it caught in her throat and sounded more like a sob.

"I never said—"

"I became an embarrassment to myself. Especially with your church friends. I didn't fit in with them, Max, no matter how hard I tried. I couldn't share their stories the way you could. I never went to their youth meetings, their parties. I wasn't part of their group. I even failed at trying to entertain them."

He remembered the New Year's Eve party she'd

begged to host, the elaborate preparations she'd gone to, how flat and lifeless it had seemed.

"So maybe we should have met new people."

"We did, remember? I still blew it and you were still embarrassed so don't pretend." Her blue eyes hardened. "I'm not the kind of person who impresses people like the ones you know, Max. We should have realized from the start that my ability as a chameleon only extends to my work."

"That's not—"

"I can't pretend to be the person you need anymore," she told him, her voice brimming with a desperation he'd never heard before. "I can't be your wife. That's what I figured out in the Outback. That's why I had the papers drawn up as soon as I got back. I knew I had to do it."

"But we made a commitment, Callie. We're married. You can't just walk away from that!" Max felt like he was slipping and couldn't regain his footing. "You can't just stop being married."

"I already have. That's why you got those papers."

"Really?" Her flat tones infuriated him. "Why now? What's the rush? Is there someone else?"

"Don't be stupid." She offered him a glance of pity. "In the Outback I had a lot of time to look at what I'd made of my life, what I'd done to yours. You need to be married to someone like one of your friends, Max. Someone who knows how things work in your circle, who's used to your way of doing things."

"It's nice to know you've decided that for both of us," he snapped, saw the icy frost over her eyes. Or maybe it was tears. "What about what I want?" he asked quietly.

"You already told me what you don't want." The

words bit into him with a pain he couldn't avoid. They were his words. "You don't want a wife who does what I do, you don't want to be married to someone who might have to leave on a moment's notice and can't guarantee when she'll return. You want the kind of life I can't live."

"Can't or won't?" He tilted her chin so he could see into her eyes.

She met his gaze. Just for an instant he thought he saw a glimmer of the person he'd fallen in love with three years ago, the girl with no past, no family, but who threw herself into love wholeheartedly.

The girl he now knew he'd never really known at all.

Callie pulled out of his grasp, rose. "I'll go make some dinner. I guess we missed lunch."

He let her go, watched through the window as she mucked about in the galley. As usual, she was focused on the moment, intent on her work. But he couldn't help wondering—did she ever think about *that* day?

"It's ready," she told him, huffing a little under the weight of the huge tray she carried up the stairs.

Max took it from her, set it on the table. Callie laid two mismatched placemats across from each other, then carefully arranged the place settings on them. He'd specifically equipped his vessel with two complete sets of tableware, one for more formal occasions, which she'd chosen to place in front of him, one plainer set, which she'd selected for herself. He opened his mouth to ask why, quickly clamped it shut. One thing he'd learned— Callie's actions were never random.

Callie always had a reason for her behavior. Only now Max was beginning to realize that most of the time he'd never bothered to find out what her reasons were. The different dishes were meant to point out the differences between them.

He sat silent. Now was hardly the time to argue. It would only emphasize her belief that she didn't fit—as she'd claimed—into his life.

Shouldn't that be *their* life?

Chagrin chewed at him as he recalled the many accommodations she'd made to fit into his life—and the few he'd made to fit his life to hers.

"Aren't you going to sit down?"

Max sat, sampled her cooking and found it as exotic as ever. The flavors were different, complex but delicious nonetheless.

"It's very good," he told her, picking up his water glass. He clinked the glass of it against her plastic tumbler. "To the cook."

"You used to say I made things too spicy. I used a lot of peppers. Is the shrimp going to bother your stomach?" she asked, her eyebrows pulled together in a furrow of concern as she sipped her water. "I guess lots of people find my food too hot."

People like who? he wanted to demand, jealousy growing inside.

But while she'd been cooking he'd rethought his confrontational approach. Callie thought their differences were too great to be overcome. Maybe it was time to help her see the similarities they shared. Max leaned back in his chair and let the flavors burst onto his tongue while he launched into phase one of his new plan to get his wife back.

"It's not too hot, Callie, nor too spicy," he told her

quietly. "It just takes a few minutes to identify the flavors hitting my tastebuds. I like it very much."

"Which is a nice way of saying you can't figure out what kind of sauce it's supposed to be." She watched his face, eyes brimming with curiosity. "Your stomach must have gotten stronger. You didn't even comment on the paprika."

Max let that pass, finished his meal, then pushed away the plate. "Nobody cooks like you, Callie," he told her sincerely.

She seemed confused by his words, as if she couldn't understand that he actually liked what she'd prepared. How humbling to realize that things he'd said and done had made her feel inadequate.

They sat in the silence as twilight fell around them. Encouraged by the fact that she didn't make some excuse to hurry below to do the dishes, Max told her stories about the dog he'd adopted, the chocolate Lab he'd named Radar.

"Why Radar?"

"He can sense table scraps coming his way at a hundred feet," he told her with a grin. "He's boarding at the vet's."

Callie's whole face seemed to soften as she stared out over the water. "I always wanted a dog," she whispered. "But where I lived, dogs weren't—"

Her cell phone rang. Max longed to beg her to ignore it, to finish what she'd been going to say. But she jumped up, hurried away from the table to dig it out of her backpack.

"Yes?" She listened for several minutes, then clicked it closed.

"Anything important?"

"An update. Finders got a report that Josiah was spotted on his way to Ketchikan. Apparently he hates staying in town so he'll probably camp out with a couple of friends for two nights and show up in Ketchikan sometime the day after tomorrow. He usually doesn't stay longer than a day."

Meaning they had to get there ASAP. Max sighed. Always her work came between them. *At least that's what he was blaming it on this time.*

He rose.

"I'll get us under way if you don't mind cleaning up this mess. Thanks for dinner, too. It was great."

"You're welcome. I'll bring you up some tea when it's ready." She watched him ascend to the upper deck. "Isn't it dangerous to sail at night?"

"We haven't got time to sail, Callie. You need to get there fast so we'll use the engines. I have radar, GPS, the whole deal installed on *Hope* so there's not much danger. If I push it, we just might make it to Ketchikan in time to meet Josiah. A good thing I had the engine upgraded when I designed this baby."

Max pulled anchor and backed them out of the cove, set his bearings and plotted his course. It was going to be tight, but there was an outside chance he could get her there by the day after tomorrow and he was taking it.

A balloon of pride lodged inside his gut as *Hope* skimmed over the smooth, flat surface of the water. His creation, his design. And they both worked beautifully. He made a small course correction, noticed a new blip on his radar. Someone else was going their way. Not unusual given they were traveling the Inside Passage.

Just for fun, he tracked starboard for a while. The blip followed. He pushed the throttle up a couple of knots. The distance between them expanded only for a few seconds, then the blip caught up. Someone was monitoring their course so closely they adjusted their own to follow.

Now that was odd.

Max wasn't sure how much time passed before Callie returned with an insulated mug of steaming hot tea. He took a sip and smiled. Sugared exactly right. "Perfect. Thank you."

"Is your headache gone?" she asked quietly.

"Yes, thanks. Whatever you gave me certainly did the trick."

She stood beside him, protected by the cabin's glass surround, facing forward as the bow cut through the water.

A soft, sweet rush of comfort filled him that she was there, beside him—until she spoke and the peace between them disintegrated like fog in sun.

"You're trying, Max. And I really appreciate that."

He noted a little tremble in her voice, saw her lick her lips, draw a deep breath.

"I didn't file for divorce lightly, but the truth we both know is that you can't forgive me for what I did. I can't forgive myself. That's why I had the papers drawn up and sent to you. Once we reach Ketchikan, I hope you'll sign them."

What she'd done? He frowned, fought to make sense of her words. Did Callie really think that she alone was responsible for whatever had gone wrong between them? He knew losing the baby had changed her, that he should have talked about it more, tried to understand what she was going through. But he'd been so angry when she'd immediately taken another assignment over-seas—he couldn't understand that. Why had she run away? Why then?

He'd told her from the beginning that he wanted a family. But after she'd taken off and stayed away, he'd begun to wonder if Callie had wanted a child—or if she'd just let him think she did.

"You're in a bit of a rush to file for divorce already, aren't you?" he asked tightly. "We haven't even tried to talk, haven't spent time trying to figure out if we can fix what's gone wrong. I think we owe our marriage that."

"There is no point in talking. You don't know me, Max. You never did. That's not your fault. It's mine, it's who I am. I'm not the kind of person you should have married. I realize that now. But I can't take any more guilt for the past. I—" She hiccupped a sob, stifled it. "I can't."

As quietly as she came, she disappeared below. Except for the well-tuned purr of the motor, all was quiet on the boat. But Max knew Callie wasn't sleeping.

The past, one tiny chunk of it, lay between them, dead, buried even, but not forgotten.

Never forgotten.

Max preferred to face life head-on, hit the hard spots and work his way through to a resolution. But to do that in this marriage he needed Callie's cooperation and it was clear she wasn't about to talk to him—not tonight, not ever—by the sounds of what she'd just said.

So what now?

He glanced at the console, noted the tiny red blip on the radar that continued to draw closer. He changed his course three times, watched the blip move three times.

This wasn't just another craft traveling the Inside Passage. Someone was deliberately following them. Why?

THREE

"Welcome to Ketchikan, Callie."

Two days of travel had brought them to the dock along a steep hillside where hints of the city peeked over the edge of piles stretched out over the water. Callie glanced around with growing curiosity.

"The city was originally a fishing camp on the outskirts of Deer Mountain," Max explained. "I suggest a visit to the Saxman Native village, where you'll see the Tlingit culture and their fantastic totem poles. If we've time, I'd love to go with you on a kayak trip later. It gives a different perspective and it's one of the best ways to see things here."

"You sound like a tour guide." Callie tied the mooring rope around the cleat as Max had shown her years ago. He followed right behind, checking no doubt. Making sure she hadn't messed up again. "I doubt there will be time for sightseeing."

"That's a shame. Can I come with you?" he asked, following her down the dock and up the steps to street level.

"I have to meet a contact. I'm not sure he'll approach if you're there. It's better if we separate."

Once they were topside, Callie paused to savor the

picturesque view as morning crowds bustled around them. Then she faced him.

"Your part of the agreement has been more than fulfilled. Thank you for bringing me here, Max. I'll be fine now. You can get on with whatever plans you had before I happened along."

The brush-off didn't work, not that she'd expected it to.

"Running away again, Callie?" His glare bit past her pitiful erected facade.

She could read that expression so easily. Anger, frustration, disappointment. Always disappointment. Like a tidal wave the guilt rushed in.

"I am not running away," she grated, struggling to suppress the rush of feelings that would swamp her if she dwelled on the thought of Max being gone from her life permanently. "I'm doing what I was sent here to do."

"Right. Well I'm not leaving here until I know you've made contact with this man and gotten whatever it is you need." Max crossed his arms over his chest. "I'll stick around until everything's arranged. If you don't mind, that is?" he added with a glare. "And even if you do, actually."

He was mad that she'd dismissed him so easily, but it was either that or let him persuade her to think about what she was losing—and Callie couldn't afford to lose her focus. Not now.

She spotted a man across the street, waiting in front of an ice cream shop like any other tourist. Her contact.

"Wait here. I'll be back in a minute." She approached the man in the big sheepskin vest, saw the crest on his pocket and mentally matched it with a picture she'd been shown at Finders. Callie pasted on a grin.

"G'day, mate. Don't s'pose you'd be able to tell me

how to get to the tourist information center in town, would you?"

"Of course. You can get a lot of maps there if you want to see the area." He pulled a map from under his arm and pretended to point out the way. "Intel thinks he'll arrive in town around five," he murmured. "You'll find directions inside. If he gets his mail he'll know someone is coming to see him, but he gets skittish around too many people so try to catch him alone."

"Okay."

He glanced around before continuing.

"Finders said there was some kind of error. You're to hand over the papers you were given and take these instead. A local lawyer drew them up." He indicated the long brown envelope under his coat.

"That's right friendly of you, mate," she said loudly as she knelt to open the zipper on her backpack. "I reckon I might have an address of where I'm headed tucked in here somewhere." She lifted out the envelope Shelby had given her, rose, held it out, accepted the other in return.

Someone bumped into her just enough to make Callie lose her balance. The package was ripped from her grasp. Before she could jump up she was shoved against the rough log siding behind her. She saw her contact fall to his knees. His hands were empty.

"'Ere now," she bellowed, trying to get a glimpse of the thief. "Where are the police when you need 'em?"

"He's been watching me for a couple of hours," her contact whispered, on his feet now. "Thought he was a pickpocket but he must have made me. You'll have to get Finders to replace those documents. I'm done." He slipped away among a group of tourists fresh off a cruise ship that had just docked.

Callie still had the map he'd given her, which was supposed to have some directions inside. She stuck that into her pack, then moved around to the side of the building where there were less people. Privacy assured, she pulled out her phone, dialed Daniel's number, waited.

"Eh, there, mate," she burst out jovially when he picked up his private line. She grinned at a passing couple. "I made it to Alaska. Yeah, mighty good trip it was, too. But some thief snatched those directions to your aunt's house. Now I haven't got a clue how to get to her place."

"You met Peter?" Daniel caught on at once.

"Great guy," she said, keeping the accent up for all she was worth. "Had to leave rather suddenly so he wasn't much help. Lost his tucker, he did."

"Both copies are gone." Daniel sounded resigned. "I understand. We'll get another set to you ASAP. Did you get a look at the guy who took them?"

"No. Tell Mum hello, will you?"

"Shelby's right here, listening."

"Some of your advice wasn't so helpful, Mum. A bit rough up here."

"Hang tight, Callie," Shelby told her. "Remember, we warned you something like this might happen. Follow the directions."

"Righto. I'll do that, Mum. Gotta go. Time to see the sights now. G'day." She clicked the phone closed, moved back to the main street and did a quick survey.

Max stood where she'd left him, though now he was leaning nonchalantly against a street lamp as if waiting for a recalcitrant wife who'd insisted on shopping longer than he liked.

"With a disguise like that, maybe he's the one who should be working for Finders," she muttered crossly as she jogged to the other side of the street.

"Oy, there. Reckon I could get you to show me where the police station is? Some dingo just ran off with my stuff."

"Sure." He straightened, took her arm. "Let's go this way."

"No, it's too public," she whispered before noticing that he was already using the flush of tourists as cover, darting in and out among them to make his way down the street.

"Let's take a side trip," she murmured and stepped inside a store filled with people who couldn't decide which kind of fudge they should choose. She led Max behind a display stand while she studied the street. "I don't see anyone," she told him.

"There was a man watching you when your tête-à-tête was broken up, but he left when your attacker did."

She blinked, shocked by his words. "A second guy? I didn't see anyone."

"You were on the ground," he reminded her. "But I was in a perfect position. A man stood down the street, watching. His attention never strayed from you." He pulled on her arm, urging her away from two eavesdropping shoppers. "Tall fellow, maybe six-two, thin as a rail. Dead eyes."

"Dead eyes?" she repeated. "What does that mean?"

"Eyes that have seen too much. I saw some of the photos you used to bring home to study," he admitted.

"They had the same look. Like a person who's lost hope that his life will change—that there is any good left in the world. I call that expression 'dead eyes.'"

Callie had always assumed Max had no interest in what she did, that he preferred hobnobbing with the wealthy well-heeled clients he spent his time wooing into buying his nautical creations. Apparently she'd been wrong. Max had seen enough of her homework to recognize a certain type of look, one Finders used to profile a target they'd been hired to find.

Knowing that Max had been alert enough to spot someone out of place here in Ketchikan when he should have been looking around like any other normal tourist surprised her. Maybe she'd misjudged him.

"I'll keep my eyes peeled," she murmured, irritated that she couldn't identify this guy. Carelessness was an agent's worst nightmare. It left the door open to too many possibilities. Maybe coming here with Max was a mistake. He drew her attention away from the case, made her think of other things, dreams that were best left dead and buried.

Callie made a decision. At the first opportunity she'd have to send him packing—whether he wanted to go or not.

"Come on. We can get out of this place here." Max led her through a door that exited onto a side street. "What now?" he asked when they were on the side-walk once more.

"I need to read my instructions. That would be easier and more private in the boat. Shelby said they'd deliver new papers. I'm guessing they'll arrive there."

"Fine."

They worked their way back to the dock. Callie heaved a sigh of relief when she was safely below. She rummaged through her pack for the information.

"How are you going to know what your man looks like, even if you do see him?" Max demanded from the galley, where the fresh scent of coffee had begun to waft forward. "As I recall, Josiah wouldn't allow himself to be photographed."

Callie nodded. "The only picture I have of him was taken more than twenty years ago. That's why I need to read this. Shelby mentioned she'd bring me up to speed as Intel came in. She's supposed to set up a contact point at the lumberjack show they hold here."

She laid out the papers the man in town had given her, speed-read them, willing her mind to absorb the information.

"Amazing," she murmured as she set down the last piece of paper, then stared at a fuzzy image of a man who looked like a long-lost professor.

"What's amazing?" Max set a cup of coffee before her, along with a ham sandwich and an apple. He stared at the photo.

"Josiah Harpnell is past seventy yet he treks from his homestead, which is somewhere up in the Yukon, to town for supplies, and does it mostly on foot. He has a snowmobile for emergencies, but other than that, he refuses to use any mechanical means, probably because of those environmental issues you mentioned."

She nodded her thanks, took a sip of the coffee he'd prepared and winced. Double strong, as usual.

"Guess I put a little too many grounds in the pot.

Sorry." Max winced as he swallowed his own coffee. "Needs more cream."

"Cream isn't going to help this coffee." She pushed her cup away, studied her papers. "According to Finders, Josiah used to have a dog team that brought him into town in winter. The rest of the information is sketchy. All they've been able to learn is that he comes into Ketchikan on an old logging road. I'll have to follow his trail to catch up with him."

"On foot?" Max had been about to sit down across from her but froze at her words. "You could be attacked again."

"Not likely." She motioned to the chair, waited till he was seated. "Think about it, Max. They've got the papers now and they can see that they're unsigned so it's doubtful that I'm any threat." She bit her lip, decided to be honest. "Whoever is behind this will probably decide that it's easier to let me find Josiah and take it from there."

"I don't like that scenario any better," he grated, his hard jaw set in that unyielding line that didn't need explaining. Max, The Protector, was jumping into the fray.

"Sorry, but I work with what they give me. Sometimes the conditions aren't what I'd choose, but I don't know the whole story yet. According to what's here, I have to show up at that lumberjack show at three to get whatever else they've got." She checked her watch. "Finders wants everything kept very low-key until I can get Josiah's signature."

"What does 'low-key' mean?"

"I can't draw attention to myself." *Which you would do.* "Shelby will have had time to get some local guy to draft new papers by then."

"I'm going with you."

"You can't! You'll spoil everything." She glared at him. "This is what I do, Max. If you're with me I won't be able to blend into the crowd and I need to do that to get more information." She lowered her voice, tried to make him understand. "Whoever was there today probably saw you, too. If they see you again, especially near me, they're going to suspect there are two of us tracking Josiah. They could come after you."

"I can take care of myself."

"Uh-uh." She shook her head, refusing to give in. "Not on my watch you can't. Daniel never agreed to it and I'm not, either. You stepped in, gave me a ride here. Fine, we've arrived. Thank you. Now you have to leave and let me get on with what I do."

"I can't, Callie." The words seemed torn from him. He dragged a hand through his dark hair as if searching for a way to explain. "I can't let things end this way. It isn't right."

"Maybe not. But it's the way it is. You're going to have to accept that." She bit her lip then forced the words out. "We should never have married. People like me don't get hooked up with men like you, Max. I'm a traveler. I like my work. I like never being tied down."

"I won't tie you down. But you're not going into this alone. I can't fathom why Daniel thought you should."

"Because he knows the situation and my abilities better than you do." She'd have to try harder to get rid of him. "Listen to me, Max. This guy who followed me—he could be dangerous. I can't afford to be watching out for you, protecting you when my focus should be on my job. There's no reason for you to be here. Go home. Build your boats. Get on with your life."

"*Our life.* And that's exactly what I'm trying to do."

She shook her head.

"Us being married doesn't work, Max. You want a wife who's content to make a home for you, someone who'll have a packet of kids, puddle in the garden, host fancy dinner parties. You have this fantasy that we'll go sailing and everything will be peachy."

"What's wrong with that?" he demanded belligerently.

"Nothing." She gentled her voice. "Except that isn't who I am. I love what I do. To me there's nothing more thrilling than starting out on a new assignment."

"Nothing?" he asked so quietly it made her blink.

"You know what I mean." She couldn't fall into the trap of remembering what they'd shared. "Repeating the past won't help. This is my life. I am who I am, Max. I don't punch a clock or sit at a desk."

"I know all of that." His face remained implacable.

"Then?" She frowned, trying to decipher the unspoken message he was sending.

"You don't have to take every job Finders Inc. offers you, do you? You can turn down some? That's part of your contract."

Suddenly she knew exactly where this was heading and wished she'd never come back to his boat.

"Why didn't you turn it down, Callie?" he whispered, his face stark with pain. "Why didn't you just say no to whatever they sent you there for? Why did you have to go to Iraq?" He stared at the tabletop, his voice so low, so filled with pain it hurt to listen. "If you hadn't gone—"

"But I did," Callie almost yelled, the pain so deep it

ripped and tore everything in its path. It took a moment to regain control. "I went, Max. I went and I lost our baby because of it. That's what you can't get past. It's there every time you look at me, every time you think I'm not watching."

Emotions rose high. It took Callie a moment to get herself under control.

"Do you think I don't know that you blame me? I blame myself. But I can't change what happened and I refuse to go on living like that."

"I just want to know, to understand. Is that so wrong?"

"Yes. Because I can't explain it to you anymore than you can tell me why you have to place a mast just so or put the cleats in a certain position." She gathered up her papers, shoved them in her backpack, then looked at him. "But even if I could make up an answer you'd like, what would change, Max? What would be different now?"

"I don't know." He sat down, shoulders slumped, face as haggard as it had been on that day her world had caved in.

"We're not the same people we were. That's part of life. You've made a career change. You started over. Good. Now it's time to make another change. Let go of the past, of whatever you thought we could have. Find someone new." The words killed her to say and as soon as they were spoken she moved, carrying the dishes to the sink, reversing her jacket so no one would recognize it, tugging on a cap and slinging her backpack over one shoulder.

"Thank you for helping me, Max," she whispered. "But there isn't anything more you can do. Go home. Get on with your life. Forget we ever had a past."

Without a backward glance, Callie climbed the stairs

to the main deck, left the boat and headed for the giant signboard she'd seen earlier. A man handed her a leaflet that told about the lumberjack show. She glanced at it, recalled the directions she'd been given and then headed in that direction, trying desperately not to think about the man she'd left behind.

Max wasn't the same man today any more than she was the same woman who'd married him. Once he'd been so full of life, so ready to take a chance at happiness, to enjoy people, to share his sense of fun and laughter. But when she looked at him now Callie wondered how long it had been since he'd really laughed.

She'd done that to him—ruined his life because of her own selfishness. She'd ruined the precious love she'd once thought she'd never find. Because of a lie—no, a bunch of lies. And because of a secret, because no matter how hard she tried, Callie Merton could never become the woman he needed. The kind of wife Max wanted didn't have secrets.

She stood at the edge of a huge sign that proclaimed "The Alaskan Lumberjack Show" and waited in line, watching as participating lumberjacks practiced racing up a pole, cutting slices from logs and throwing axes as if they were darts.

She bought her ticket and moved to the left, into the lineup of those who also wanted to see the show, but preferred to sit up front. If only she could figure out who this contact would be she'd have a better idea of what to look for and maybe that would tell her where to sit.

A large group of seniors flooded through the entrance and pushed past, pressing her against a stockade that had been formed around the arena to prevent unpaying customers from seeing the show.

Callie breathed in relief when they finally moved and she was in the open again, but it caught in her throat as an ax whizzed toward her. She dodged sideways, but not quickly enough. She flinched at the bite of it through her down-filled jacket, almost passed out at the pain as it sliced through the skin of her shoulder and pinned her jacket to the wall. A moment later a hand reached out, pressed her other shoulder hard against the stockade.

"You want to watch what you get mixed up in here, lady. Forget Josiah Harpnell and get out of Ketchikan."

His toque was pulled low, she couldn't quite see his face as he cupped her cheek in his hand, but his thumb was rough and he jerked her head to one side, crushing her face against the pickets. Callie gasped at the pain that radiated through her shoulder, fought through another wave of dizziness.

"Or?" she whispered, daring him to say it.

"Or next time he won't let you walk away."

"Who's 'he'?" she asked. But the man was gone.

She had to get free, follow him, but Callie could not move the embedded ax. A crowd was gathering, preventing her from seeing where the man went. She tried to move the ax again, groaned.

"Let me." Max's face swam into focus.

"You're not supposed to be here," she grated, forcing the words out.

"Yeah, yeah. So sue me." He examined the situation. "A flesh wound, but it's going to hurt," he told her as he grasped the handle.

"It already does." She gritted her teeth as he pulled

the blade free, glad to wrap her good arm around his waist for support as the world started spinning.

"You'd better get her to the hospital to get that looked at," a quiet voice murmured behind her left ear.

"Don't worry. I intend to." Max would have dragged her forward, but Callie refused to move.

"Wait," she whispered, leaning against him. "Wait a minute."

"Here are some tourist papers you might want to read while you're recuperating." The man handed her a carefully folded newspaper. "Helps pass the time." He stepped forward to whisper, "Be careful." Then with a glance at Max he pushed his way through the crowd and was gone.

Minutes later officials arrived, heard their story and took them both to the hospital. Callie was ushered to an examining room immediately.

"I'll handle the paperwork," Max told her when a nurse suggested he leave. He took her backpack, tucked the newspaper inside and slung it over his shoulder. "All of it."

"Thanks." She had little energy for anything else and the next half hour passed in a blur.

Max reappeared just as the doctor fastened the last stitch in place. "How deep?"

"What are you doing in here?" the doctor demanded.

"Checking on my wife."

"Okay. Well, it's mostly a surface wound. I put in a couple of stitches just to hold it together. If she's careful it should heal nicely."

"She's never careful," Max said, eyes flashing as he glared at Callie.

"I see. In that case I'll give you this topical antibiotic. Apply it twice a day. If there's inflammation or redness, get her back in here tomorrow."

"Excuse me, I can hear and understand everything you're saying, you know." Callie snatched the tube. "I'll apply the ointment myself."

The doctor finished wrapping gauze around her shoulder, taped it in place. "No stress, no strain on the arm or shoulder. Let Mother Nature do her work. And let your husband take care of you. He can handle whatever needs doing."

"See, I told you," Max quipped.

Callie shot him a glare that did nothing to quell the glint in his eyes.

"Sleep is going to be tough tonight, young lady. I'll write you a prescription for some pain medication."

"I'll make sure she takes it." Max held out his hand. "Thanks."

"Yeah." The doctor shook his hand then left to get his prescription pad. Only then did Callie realize her shirt was half off, Max could see her cotton camisole. She half turned away to hide but he refused to move.

"Stop being such a prude," he told her, a sardonic smile tipping up his mouth. "I've seen your shoulder before. Besides, you need help. Here. I'll hold it, you try and slip your arm in. Okay?"

It took a Herculean effort not to burst into tears at the soft, gentle tone in his voice, even more not to lay her head on his shoulder and just rest when she finally got her arm in. Callie let him button her shirt, forced herself to keep breathing when his knuckles brushed the sensitive skin of her neck.

It's not a romantic gesture, you stupid woman, she told herself. He's just being kind. Which made it even worse.

"Now your jacket." Max seemed unaware of her inner turmoil. He waited patiently while she fought to do it herself, then without saying a word gently eased the shredded material over her aching shoulder. A moment later his hands circled her waist and he lifted her off the table. "Can you walk?"

"Of course." She glared at him. "I'm not made of fairy dust."

"Feels like it. You've lost at least twenty pounds."

"I was too heavy."

"Liar." He met her glare, face impassive, followed her to the desk and accepted the prescription.

"Thank you," she said to the doctor.

He nodded.

"That's my job." He winked at Max. "She'll stop being so stubborn when the pain kicks in. Until then, my advice is to just wait."

"That's something I'm getting used to doing," Max grumbled, but his eyes were on Callie and for once she struggled to hide her innermost thoughts.

"You can fill that in the pharmacy over there."

It took only a few moments to get the pills. Outside the hospital Max motioned a taxi forward, helped her inside.

"Are you all right?" he asked when she laid her head back and closed her eyes.

"Yes." She sat up straight, stared ahead.

"You're sure?" He was frowning, as if he didn't quite believe her.

"Don't fuss, Max."

"Right. Wouldn't want to fuss about a tiny thing like

an ax in the shoulder." He ordered the taxi to the harbor where they'd moored. "I gave a preliminary report at the hospital, but shouldn't you talk to the police, give them a better description?"

"I will. But later, not right now."

Callie eased herself out of the taxi, followed him down the dock wishing she'd taken one of the pain pills before she'd left the hospital as the doctor had advised. Sometimes the tough act wasn't easy to keep up.

Max jerked to a stop and she bumped into him, squealed at the pain of contact against his hard body.

"What are you—oh, no!"

His boat, *Hope*, his precious new sailboat was a ragged mess of broken glass, battered hull, damaged fiberglass and torn loungers. The mainsail would have to be replaced, the sails refitted, the deck repaired. Whoever had done it hadn't bothered with neatness. She could see through the gaping hole that the galley had been torn apart, contents strewn everywhere. The damage was extensive.

"Oh, Max, I'm so sorry I got you into this." She could have wept at the look covering his lean, hard face. "I'm sorry. I'm so sorry."

"It's just a boat," he said after a long silence. "I can always build another. At least we weren't on it." He took one last look, then turned his back on the devastation, grasped her hand and led her away.

"Where are we going?"

"We'll get a hotel for tonight. I'm not leaving you alone, Callie. While you rest, I'm going to have another chat with the police. This was no accident. Someone is trying to send you a message."

"What do you mean?"

"I didn't tell you and I should have. I apologize."

"Tell me what?"

"Someone followed us. I tracked them on the boat's radar, tried to get rid of them. They followed every move and when I followed you today I led them right to you."

"No, you didn't, Max." This was not his fault. "Someone was following me in Victoria."

"I should have lost them at sea. Or at least let you know. That ax could have severed your arm." His face blanched. "I thought I could handle things but I never imagined someone would go to these ends—"

She'd never seen him like this. Callie touched his arm.

"I'm fine, Max. Or I will be after I get some rest." She shrugged. "It's all part of the job."

"Getting attacked? Maybe you should rethink your vocation." His eyes grew icy.

"Max, I appreciate—" She'd wanted to thank him for handling things for her but he mistook her meaning, held up a hand, his face angry.

"Don't bother saying it because there is no way I'm leaving this place without you. You want to find this guy, fine. But I'll be right here with you." He flagged a taxi, held open the door. "Don't argue with me, Callie, because this time we're doing it my way."

I wasn't going to argue, she wanted to tell him. *I was going to thank you.*

But as the car sped along the street she was glad she hadn't said it. It would be a stupid thing to say. What had she done but ruin yet another thing Max loved? Thanks to her his beautiful boat was gone. In a strange way it now seemed obvious that his *Hope* should be smashed to bits—just like their marriage.

Max was right—*things* could be fixed. What he hadn't accepted was that people couldn't.

If whoever had done this had found him on board, he might be dead by now. She couldn't stand to think it, but she had to. She had to look at this from every angle.

Someone didn't want her to find Josiah Harpnell and they were willing to go to extreme lengths to stop it.

As the cab roared through the streets, Callie faced her worst fear.

If Max stayed, she could be endangering his life.

Somehow she had to get him to leave.

FOUR

With tourist season still running full tilt, Max found it difficult to procure a hotel room.

Finally they found a small place that had a vacancy. The tiny room with only one bed would not have been Callie's first choice, he was certain of that. But she was too worn-out to complain and there was nothing else available.

Once he'd rolled back the bedspread, she slid off her tattered jacket, pushed off her shoes and climbed in. She meekly accepted a glass of water and a small white pill without comment.

"I'll just rest for a few minutes," she murmured, handing him the glass. Her thick eyelashes dropped against her pale cheeks. "Then you can have the bed. I'll take the couch."

He didn't bother arguing because she was asleep.

Moving into the bathroom, Max pulled out his phone and dialed the police to report his damaged boat. His body felt beaten when he replayed the scene of carnage in his mind but that was nothing compared to the damage that could have been done if Callie had been on board.

It was obvious someone already knew they were

together. That worked in his favor because he had no intention of leaving her here alone.

"Thanks very much. I'll stop by your office as soon as I can." A noise from the adjoining room penetrated. Max ended the conversation, pushed open the door. Callie lay on the bed, her head thrashing from side to side as she murmured something. He moved closer to hear.

"Not my baby," she whimpered. "Please God, not my baby."

An arrow of stark agony pierced his heart at the remembered pain of those dashed hopes. When she didn't settle, he reached out, brushed the tousled curls from her smooth forehead. The pills must be making her dream.

"It's okay, Callie. The baby's in Heaven."

"Really?" she asked, her voice so quiet he had to lean nearer to hear.

She was awake now, eyes huge in her gaunt face. Though she drew back from his touch, their intensity seemed to beg him to ease the pain he saw shimmering in those ocean-blue depths.

"How can you be so sure?"

"I just know. I believe God cares for those who can't care for themselves. Our baby's being cared for by angels."

It hurt to say it, hurt even more to think of all they'd lost. Like a current finally bubbling to the surface, his question burst out.

"Why did you go, Callie? Can't you tell me now? Please?"

"No." Like a clam her face closed up, regained that cold, vacant expression she used to shield her thoughts. "It's the past. Let it go, Max."

"I can't." He rose, stared at her. "Can't you understand? One day I had everything I ever wanted. Then you left without any explanation. The next thing I knew our child was gone and you wouldn't come back." He touched her uninjured shoulder, desperate for answers. "I need to know why."

"Ask your God why," she whispered bitterly before she turned her face away.

Max felt the way his boat had looked—smashed, damaged beyond repair. He could almost feel the last vestige of hope he'd clung to for the past few months wither and slide away.

"I thought we loved each other." The words burst out of him like a dam that had been breached. "I thought you meant it when you said 'till death do us part.'"

She flashed a sorrowful glance at him but he pressed on in spite of the pain he knew he was causing both of them.

"Maybe I was the only one doing the loving in this relationship. Was I a game to you, Callie? Was our marriage only something to pass the time between jobs?"

Callie sat up.

"How can you say that?" she demanded, voice choked.

"I say it because you're ready to throw away everything without telling me why, and I need to know. I have a right to know." Max thought he was making progress until he added the last bit.

She turned away from him. "I'm tired, Max. I need to sleep. Please, just leave me alone. Go home if you want to. Forget about me. I'll be fine."

He wanted to argue, to make her feel the searing anguish that ripped apart his insides. But how could you argue with someone who refused to fight, someone, moreover, who looked as if she was ready to cry?

"I'm going downstairs. I'll be back in a while with something for you to eat." Max touched her cheek, waited for her to look at him. "We are going to talk, Callie. Sooner or later we *are* going to talk."

"Later then," she whispered, her voice low and husky. "Please, make it later."

He nodded, left the room. But as he walked down the two flights Max began making other plans. Callie might think she could push him away by refusing to discuss what had happened, but he wasn't going to give up that easily. Maybe this was his last chance to make her see what she was throwing away. Well then—he intended to use whatever means was at hand.

He pulled out his phone.

"Daniel? Sorry to bother you so late. I've got a favor to ask."

Callie waited until Max's footsteps died away, until there was no one to see. Then she slipped from the bed, retrieved her backpack from a chair and pulled out an envelope from a compartment hidden inside.

Fingers trembling, she drew out the black-and-white photograph, let the tears cascade down her face as she brushed a fingertip against the round head, the small curled fingers, the tiny bent legs.

"If you're there," she whispered, forcing the words past the lump in her throat. "If you're really there, God, please take care of my little baby. For Max's sake."

The same old pain welled up until she felt as if her heart would rip apart. Gone. Lost. This baby was supposed to be their future—hers and Max's—something to draw them closer. Until she'd ruined even that.

Callie slid the ultrasound picture back inside the envelope and tucked it into her pack. Then she crawled back into bed, grabbed the vial and swallowed another pill.

Then she waited for the pill to obliterate the empty, aching hole in the depths of her soul.

When the knock came at the door the next morning, Callie stepped out of the bathroom, glanced at Max, nodded.

"You can answer it," she whispered.

He pulled the door open, accepted the delivery of a thick envelope bearing the Finders watermark.

"It's for you," he told her. While he moved the tray with their breakfast things off the table and into the hallway Callie sat down, slit open the package and studied the contents.

"Copies of the documents I need to get signed." She set aside those papers, studied the information underneath, then rubbed her temples.

"What's wrong?"

"Apparently yesterday's Intel came from an outside source. Looks like it was wrong. Finders confirms Josiah was spotted outside of Juneau, not Ketchikan. They think he's going to visit someone there. I'm supposed to get there right away. Which is going to be a little difficult considering Juneau isn't accessible by road. Guess I'll fly."

"Daniel called earlier. He said there aren't any flights available." Max had his back turned so Callie couldn't see his expression. "I told him I'd take you on the boat."

She frowned. "You think it's going to run despite all that damage?"

"No." He met her stare. A secret lay hidden in those brooding eyes. "Daniel sent another boat. A mutual friend of ours owns it. It should be docked, stocked and waiting for us."

"You're working with Finders now, Max?" she asked skeptically.

"I'm trying to help." His chin jutted out, telling her without words that he'd brook no refusal of his offer.

Callie opened her mouth to argue but the protest died in her throat. If Daniel had okayed Max's participation, she could hardly override those orders. Obviously her bosses wanted to get the papers signed as quickly as possible and would take whatever steps needed to ensure that happened.

Only why did it have to be Max?

With a sigh of resignation she grabbed her backpack, slid her arms into the new jacket he'd bought her, wincing at the sting of stitches.

"I'm ready whenever you are."

"I had some of my stuff moved to the boat. You didn't have anything so I asked Shelby to have someone buy a few things for you." He pulled on his own jacket and held open the door. "The tank should be filled so we can leave immediately. Are you feeling all right?"

"Fine." She avoided the hand he would have placed under her elbow and stepped into the elevator. "The sooner we get going, the sooner you'll be able to go home."

Max didn't answer, but then she hadn't expected him to.

At the harbor they found the boat waiting for them. It was big and elegant and looked impressive but it lacked the tailored clean lines of Max's *Hope*. Not that looks mattered. As long as it would run, it was fine. Callie waited while Max checked it out below then, at his beckon, climbed aboard.

"Do you want me to help you get under way? I'm not totally useless."

"You need to rest that shoulder. Besides, I'd rather get familiar with her on my own." Max's attention lay elsewhere. His focus rested on the helm and the console at the front of it. "If I need help, I'll yell."

"Okay. I'll go over my notes again." She took a seat where the sunshine was strongest and pulled out the information Shelby had sent. But a few moments later her phone interrupted.

"Callie? Hold on." Shelby said something to someone else then came back on the line. "Have you left Ketchikan?"

"Just pulling out of the harbor."

"There's a problem in Juneau. A small plane crashed at the airport and has caused a lot of problems. I've been told it would be better not to sail into the harbor while they're still dealing with that. Security is very tight. Might as well take your time getting there."

"Harpnell?"

"As far as we know he's still visiting a friend. If we're lucky he'll be there a while. You should be okay if you can get in sometime tomorrow night."

"Understood."

"Is everything okay, Callie? You sound—strange. You're not suffering too much from yesterday's attack?"

Shelby's concern sent a warm rush of gratitude through her. On one hand, Callie longed to leave Finders

Inc. behind, along with all the memories it held for her, but on the other, these were her friends. Where would she ever find a job with bosses half as wonderful?

"I'm fine. A little stiff and sore but that will pass."

"And Max?"

Callie swallowed. What could she tell them? That the fun-loving man she'd married, the one they considered almost as much a part of the Finders family as her, still hadn't forgiven her? That it was unlikely he ever would? That she'd abused the love and trust he'd placed in her and he was hurting?

"Max is fine, too. Tell Daniel thanks for the boat."

"Daniel? Oh, yeah. Daniel. Will do. Take care, Callie."

She clicked the phone closed, found Max staring down at her.

"Anything wrong?" he called.

"We don't have to hurry too much. Shelby says to plan on arriving tomorrow night." Because of the dark glasses he wore she couldn't see how that went down. "Is that okay?"

He nodded.

"We can take a look at Tracy Arm. The icebergs should still be calving." Max met her stare for one long moment before he returned to his controls.

Calving. The word made her think of babies, wrecking her determination to be cool, controlled. Callie used the excuse to stow her things below while she fought to get her emotions under control.

Why did the pain still seem so fresh even after ten months?

Below decks felt too confining. Callie stayed there as long as she could but she had to get air. They were moving quickly now. Since her new jacket wasn't the warmest and she'd only brought the most basic of gear along, Callie turned to Max's closet, searched until she found one of his thick sweaters, the kind his mother loved to knit.

Her stomach lurched at the familiar spicy after-shave clinging to the wool. That scent painted a dazzling panorama of memories—fires at the beach on a summer's night, the last ski trip before spring melted the mountain, snuggled against Max's chest watching a wee tyke talk to Santa. Why couldn't—no!

Callie fought for control. When she finally went up on deck her expression was firmly schooled in place. She wore two layers of her own clothes.

"Do you want to eat your lunch up there?" she called.

Max shook his head. "No, I'll take a break."

She waited for him on the rear of the craft, at the small table that linked into the metal connection on the floor.

"I see you figured this thing out."

"Boats are all pretty much the same, aren't they?" she muttered, then bit her lip at his pained howl. "Sorry. Guess that wasn't very tactful."

"Not for the wife of a guy who earns his living trying to make each one look and maneuver differently from anything else on the market, it isn't."

The wife of—but she wasn't his wife anymore. Hadn't been for a long time, if he'd only admit it.

Callie glanced up, realized that Max was thinking the same thing. She pushed his salad toward him to cover the awkward stretch of silence.

"How long is it since you've been up this way?" she asked, spearing a lettuce leaf she'd slathered in dressing.

"Not since last year. It was too hectic this spring for me to take off."

Because he'd sold his business.

"What will your father do now?"

Max paused in the act of lifting his salad to his lips, stared at her.

"You're kidding, right? Don't you remember his addiction to golf? He and Mom spent most of the winter in Florida. They came back for Christmas so—"

So he wouldn't be alone. Because she'd been on the other side of the world.

"Sorry," he muttered. "It's hard to talk without treading on toes, isn't it?"

Max pushed away the half-eaten salad, popped the top on his soda can. "Anything new on Harpnell?"

"They don't know any more than they did. Intel is that he's still at his friend's and we're to proceed to Juneau. We've got an extra day now, though. There's some damage to the airport tower from a crash—electrical damage I guess. No flights in or out till day after tomorrow. Shelby says security's got the place in lockdown mode. At least we don't have to rush."

"That's one good thing. I mean, if you can't get to Josiah, no one else can either."

"Unless they come by water," she mused.

"Or unless they're already there." Max stretched out his legs until his feet were resting on a bench. He tipped back his head so the sun flooded his face. "I hope he's okay. The stuff that I read about Josiah said he's a peace-loving man, doesn't like confrontation. I guess that's why he lives where he does."

"Maybe." Callie finished her meal, tasted the soda

and found it wasn't what she wanted. "I made some tea earlier. Do you want some?"

"Sure. Up there." He jerked a thumb to the control cabin, tucked his can into the holder on the table then vaulted up the steps. A moment later the engine revved and they were slipping through the glassy water again, their bow spearing a path that veered slightly from left to right as he avoided shoals and hidden or shallow reefs.

Callie went below to fetch two covered mugs. She'd just begun climbing up the ladder when she heard him yell her name.

"Come quick!"

She raced up to the main deck, heart in her mouth as she surveyed him from head to foot. He wasn't hurt, in fact he was grinning as if he'd just struck gold. "What are you yelling about?"

"Come up here."

She climbed the steps, frowned at him. "What?"

He put a hand on her shoulder, turned her so she was standing in front of him, facing the ocean. "Just look at that, Cal," he murmured, his head inclined away from shore.

The old familiar nickname pricked a sensitive chord. Callie ignored it, followed his stare. Huge black humpback whales swam through the waves in a parallel course to theirs. Black fantails flicked up crystal water droplets, which sparkled in the sunshine before they dropped back to meld into the sea.

"Aren't they something?"

"Fantastic," she agreed, awed by the massive mammals. Occasionally she caught a glimpse of several smaller whales, but they were protected by the rest of the pod and never swam far from their mothers. Even whales had enough sense to protect their children.

"I never get tired of seeing them." Max's low voice breathed, his breath brushing past her ear, soft and reverent. "They remind me how big God is, big enough to create and care for whales."

Callie moved two steps away, handed him a cup. "Here's your tea."

"Thanks." He took a drink. "We're making good time. I reckon we won't have any trouble achieving your deadline."

"That's good." She sipped from her own cup feeling awkward and uncomfortable in such close proximity. And yet there was a certain rightness about standing up here beside him, where she'd stood so many times before. Callie risked a sideways glance.

Max stared ahead, over the water, expression hidden behind the dark lenses.

"Deadlines and emergencies don't seem so important out here, do they?" he murmured. "Once you're skimming across the water, the wind seems to blow away all the unnecessary stuff and you can concentrate on what's really important."

A particular note in his voice made her regard him more thoroughly, recall the times he'd disappeared and never said where he'd been. She'd never had to ask, she'd always known he'd been sailing.

"Is that why you used to go out so often?" Callie was careful to keep any hint of reluctance from her voice. "To think?"

"Yes. Sometimes I used to get so busy holding all the

reins. I began to wonder if I'd notice if one slipped out of my hands. In my head I think I'd known for a while that I didn't want to follow in my father's footsteps. It took me a little longer to figure out why and decide what I did want to do."

"So you decided to focus on design." Design had always been an integral part of Max's love of the craft. She remembered how fondly he'd handled *Hope* and wondered if he blamed her for the boat's demise.

"After some soul-searching, yes, I did decide that," he admitted. "I like the independence of it. If I want to take a day off, I can disappear and no one cares."

Meaning her? Callie glanced across the dark blue water, remembered how quickly it could change, blow up into a gale of fury. She swallowed hard.

"What if something happened? How would anyone know where you were? You shouldn't go out alone, Max. It isn't safe."

His head turned, he lifted his glasses to peer at her. "Would you worry about me, Callie?"

"Of course. I wouldn't want anyone to be lost at sea."

"Anyone. Right." His expression lost some of its joy but after a moment he regained his usual equanimity, pointed toward the shore. "Do you see them?"

"No." She squinted across the dazzling water toward shore. "What?"

"There. Behind that little island. They've been ducking in and out for a while now, trying to stay behind us, out of sight."

"They?" Callie felt the hairs on the back of her neck rise.

"I can't identify them from this distance and if I take

the time to move alongside they'll probably take off. Anyway, I don't think chatting with us is what they have in mind." Max kept his focus on her. "I'm pretty sure they're following us."

"Why?"

"Maybe they don't have the sources you have and aren't quite sure where Josiah is. Maybe they're hoping you'll lead them to him. I don't know, Callie. Whoever it is, they are managing to keep pace with us."

"So running away isn't an option." She leaned against the wall, trying to think it through. "What do we do?"

"We keep going, take our little side trip to check out Tracy Arm and try to lose them somehow."

"And when we stop for the night?" she asked, trying to fathom his expression. "What then?"

"My suggestion would be not to stop." He held up his hand at her protest. "I don't need a lot of sleep, Cal. I'll keep going."

"You'll be too tired."

"Well, I suppose you could refresh your skills and take a turn at the wheel." He waited for her to refuse. "This one isn't the same as ours was, of course, but some things stay the same."

Callie thought it over, decided she didn't want Max to manage this for her. Yes, she had to rely on his sailing skill. He was the expert, after all. But she'd piloted boats a few times back in their old days. She could do it again, if she was very careful.

"Show me the differences."

They went through it several times until Callie thought he'd never turn the wheel over to her. Once he did, she found she liked the feeling of being in control, of knowing that if she kept to the direction he'd set them on, they'd make it through.

"I could do this for a while now if you want to rest," she offered.

Max laid his hand on top of hers, his smile weak. "I don't think so." He moved her hand away.

"Why not? I can do it, you know. I'm not totally stupid."

"I never said you were." His eyes narrowed, his face tightened and a tiny tic appeared in his neck. "Why do you have to see everything as a challenge?"

"Because it usually is," she shot back.

"Not with me. You should know I'd never challenge your ability. I more than most people know that you can do anything you set your mind to." He held her gaze. "I'm on your side, Cal. But we have to negotiate some tricky water before we can pick up our speed. I'd prefer to do that before night falls."

"I thought you knew this route like the back of your hand?" She frowned, tried to figure out what Max wasn't saying.

"I do. But I haven't been up this way for a while and I'm not taking any chances on a current shift, especially not with someone else's craft." He pointed to the GPS device. "I'll use that to get us through but I have to do it myself."

"Sorry. I didn't realize there was a navigation difficulty." She felt childish, petulant.

"Listen to me. You need to get to Juneau. I promise that we'll get there and you'll do some of the piloting along the way. But after I get us through the tough stuff. Okay?"

It was the first time in a very long time that he'd

waited for her to agree to his plans. Callie saw the flicker of hope in his eyes and realized that he wanted to make this journey as stress-free as possible. So did she, so she nodded her agreement.

"Okay. Just tell me when you want me to take over." She took a second look behind, saw the small silver boat ever so silently closing the distance between them. Whoever it was, she hoped they'd stay back, at least for a while.

"Maybe the best thing would be for you to stick around up here and watch. If you see me do something you don't understand, ask. I want you to feel perfectly comfortable at all times."

The hours flew by as Callie watched, listened and tried to absorb the wealth of information he tossed her way. Some of it she remembered from trips they'd taken together, some was totally unexpected and some she didn't understand, but by the time evening fell, she was more confident than she'd ever been about operating this sailboat, even if they had yet to hoist the mainsail.

"Want to try it on your own for a while?" he asked, one eyebrow lifted.

Callie nodded eagerly. "Are you going to lie down?"

"No. You know I can never sleep unless it's totally dark. Anyway, I want to see if I can get a better look at who's behind us." He opened a lid on the dash and withdrew binoculars. "Maybe if we can identify the boat, you can pass on the info and find out who owns it. I'm sure that's not a tough thing for Finders Inc. given their resources."

Callie concentrated on keeping their boat on course while Max scoured the water.

"Is something wrong?" she asked at last when it seemed he'd never stop staring at the water.

"I don't know."

She twisted to look over one shoulder. "What do you mean?"

"It's gone."

"Gone?" She scanned the water behind them, saw nothing. "Gone where?"

"I don't know. There are a hundred little coves, nooks and crannies galore where it could have stopped. But I don't like it." He moved the glasses, formed a semicircle covering vast areas of open ocean. "I don't like it at all."

"Why?" Max wasn't given to nervousness so this cautious side of him was surprising. "You'd think you'd be glad to see they're not there."

"You think so, Callie?" He lowered the glasses fractionally, peered at her. "I think I'd rather have my enemies in plain sight."

There was a double meaning buried there but Callie decided it was most prudent to ignore it.

"Maybe they're not enemies," she offered as she adjusted the wheel to correct their path. "Maybe we were wrong about that."

"Maybe." Max did not sound convinced. But he did glance at the compass and grinned. "You still have a tendency to veer to port," he told her as he made the correction. "That much hasn't changed. I wonder why that is."

"Sheer perversity, I expect."

"Uh-huh." He frowned, pushed a length of hair from her eyes. "The other night, when you were dreaming, you were talking about your father."

"Was I?" She kept her attention front and center.

"You've never spoken about him very much. He was an ambassador, wasn't he?"

"At one time. Mostly he was involved in the diplomatic service." She so did not want to go back to those days. "I never lived in the States until I was twelve and by then I guess I was too different."

"I remember you said something once—you had a hard time as a teen, didn't you? Why?"

"Oddball in Europe, weirdo in America." She shrugged. "It wasn't a recipe for fitting in."

"In all the time I've known you, I never met your father. Why was that?"

She swallowed, hard, stared straight ahead and strove for composure. "Leave it alone, Max."

"I can't, Callie. I need to know something about your past."

"Why?" She forced the tremble out of her voice and glared at him. "Why now?"

"Because it might help."

She felt her lips twist. "Talking about my father won't help, Max."

"How do you know? Maybe if—"

"It won't help because he's dead. Because I was never what he wanted." The words spilled out in her rush to stop him from going on. "Because my father hated me. Because the past is finished and I don't want to talk about it anymore." She couldn't keep her voice from cracking.

"Cal, you can't just stuff down whatever is painful and force yourself to forget it. The past always affects our future, even though we might not want it to."

"That's rich, coming from you." She hooked the steering into automatic pilot then turned to face him. "How has the past affected your life, Max? Tell me. You had a perfect childhood, you never rebelled, never made them ashamed of you." She gulped, forced herself to continue. "You've got great parents, you're doing the job you love, everything's going your way. So don't preach to me, okay? I don't want to hear it."

"I think you missed some parts."

"Yeah? Like what?"

"I never had a perfect childhood, Callie. And I messed up more times than you could count. The difference is that when I realized that God loved me, that He forgave me, then I learned that I had to forgive myself for my mistakes."

"Easier said than done for some of us."

"Why?" He leaned against the console opposite her, his forehead pleated in a frown. "What could you have possibly done that was so terrible that you actually believe your own father hated you?"

"I believe it because that's what he said."

"What?" Max sounded shocked. "You must have heard him wrong."

"Trust me, I didn't." Callie stared straight ahead, refused to say more.

"I'm sure you're wrong," he told her. "But even if you're not, I wish you'd chosen to discuss this with me at some time other than now."

Confused, she turned her head to look at him. "Why?"

"Because someone's coming. And by the sound of that motor I don't think they're interested in making friends."

"What will they do?"

"Try to swamp us? I don't know." His fingers closed around hers. "I'll take the wheel. You hang on."

FIVE

"I see them. Go!"

Callie pointed, then gripped the railing as he shoved the motor into high. She grinned, her blue eyes glittering with excitement.

"They can try to outrun us, or they can go into hiding again. It's their choice. Either way, I don't much care. Just do your thing and get us out of here."

His wife's confidence in him was refreshing but Max had some doubts about the viability of both options. At one time he'd taken pride in his ability to outrun anything that offered a challenge. But that had been with his own boat, on his own turf. Though he'd done some designs for this boat, it was by no means a racing craft. If he pushed too hard the motor might overheat and then they'd be late getting to Juneau.

"It's wearing the name *Windchaser*," she yelled, feet braced against the deck as she peered through the binoculars. "I can see two men on deck."

Windchaser—that was hardly unique.

"Have you got your phone? Can you call Finders and ask them to try and trace it?" He felt the hard smack of waves against the hull and tried to recall the exact specifications of its strength. "Maybe you can take another look—see if you can identify some numbers under the name."

She checked.

"Nothing there." Callie pulled out her phone, dialed and began speaking, then stopped. "Connection's no good," she muttered. "I'll try text-messaging but—"

"We've got a fax on board and our own satellite access. Look in there." Max pointed to a section on the dash, grateful that the boat's owner was a businessman who never left home without some way to contact his office. "Finders can fax us as soon as they learn something."

"Okay." Callie punched in the information quickly then slid her phone into one of the watertight compartments while they waited for a response.

Her face drew tight with tension. Max yearned to reassure her, but the truth was they were sitting ducks out here. He'd made sure there was a gun on board and Callie no doubt had one, but that didn't reassure him much. One bullet to the gas tank and they'd be flotsam. He began to pray.

"I can't hear what you're saying." She leaned closer, face puzzled. "Do you want me to do something?"

He shook his head, leaned in so his lips were next to her ear. "I'm praying. We're going to need some help out of this one."

His didn't need to look behind. His radar showed the other vessel closing in fast—the heading was exactly the same as theirs.

Callie silently monitored the situation for half an hour as the distance between the two boats closed.

"Can't you outrun them?" she asked, her frustration showing.

Max shook his head, checked the navigation indicators and moved closer to shore.

"Don't want to push too hard." *Lord, can You send us a lifeline?*

"Looks like we're running into a storm." She pointed to the looming clouds ahead. "Those clouds are awfully dark."

"That's what we want." He cut back the engine slightly and edged even closer to the shore.

"We want a storm? While we're on the water?" She raised one eyebrow at him, her curiosity obvious.

But Max could find no fear in Callie's eyes. Was that because she trusted him or because she had some other plan in mind?

"We definitely want a storm, Cal. Especially if there's fog along with it." He concentrated on the instruments, chose the most intricate course he dared.

"You're playing hide-and-seek," she guessed after watching him for several minutes.

"Yes. If we can sneak in and out of a couple more coves, maybe we can get free. Or lie low." *Until they try to board us.* He knew it was pointless to bother pretending when her chin thrust up. Callie understood exactly what he wasn't saying.

"What do you want me to do?" she asked.

"Make sure everything's fastened down below. Don't leave anything loose, just in case we get tossed around a bit." He glanced up as a clap of thunder boomed over the water, saw her blanch. "We're going to be all right, Callie. I've been praying."

"Yeah. Right." She gave him a look that didn't need translation, then turned. "I'll go below and make sure we're secure."

"Callie?"

She froze, twisted her head to stare at him.

"Are you going to be all right? As I remember, rough water was never your thing. Maybe you should take one of those pills and sleep it off."

"I'll be fine." Her shoulders squared, she met his scrutiny head-on. "I've got a job to do and I intend to do it. Whatever it takes."

"Good." He watched her until the tousled head disappeared, but once she was gone he whispered a prayer for her safety. If nothing else he'd just been reminded that a routine mission for Finders Inc. could become anything but—which had always been his worst nightmare.

What had happened with her father? And why had she never told him anything about it? Max peered through the rain, puzzling over it. Was that why God had brought them together again—so he could finally begin to understand the wife he hardly knew?

Max glanced behind him, watched the boat moving closer.

"It's not going to happen, boys," he said through gritted teeth and pressed down on the throttle firmly as sheets of rain obliterated everything around them.

He'd have to pay close attention to the instruments now, but that was all right. God had brought them this far, He'd see them through the storm.

"I've been praying."

As if that would help. A pinch of anger bit her heart. If God was going to do something, what was He waiting for?

Callie quickly dried the dishes, tucked them into their cabinets, then made sure the door locks were fastened. Once everything in the galley was in place, she checked the portholes. Wet, but not too rough. So far, so good.

The smell of rain filled her nostrils, a fresh, clean scent signaling a fresh new world. Too bad that couldn't happen with life.

She pulled her rain jacket out of her pack and thrust her arms into it. Max had his jacket up there, but maybe he'd want a hot drink later. She made coffee, filled two thermoses, added some cookies in a plastic bag then climbed topside.

Standing under the awning, Callie surveyed the ocean beyond. In Bangkok, climatologists had a word for rain like this—a tropical depression. The Inside Passage could hardly be called the tropics, but rain poured down in the same sheetlike fashion creating a leaden gray effect that seemed impenetrable.

Suddenly the engine cut back. Callie used the moment to sprint across the wet deck and duck inside the control cabin. Max swung round to look at her, his face grim.

"What's wrong?" It had to be something. Max didn't worry about incidentals. "Did we hit something?"

He shook his head, tapped a knuckle against the console. "I think we're out of fuel."

She leaned toward him, saw the needle pointing toward Full. "But—"

"It's wrong, Callie." He glanced at her, grimaced. "We've got an auxiliary, don't worry. It'll take me a few minutes to make the changeover, but for the moment I'd prefer to use our momentum to angle in toward shore. Maybe we can try and escape detection. If they're listening for sounds, they won't be able to hear where we are."

He didn't wait for her approval but began twisting the wheel right then hard left as they bobbed on the water. Callie took the chair beside him, stored the thermos and cups in a holder and prepared to wait while Max coordinated the GPS and the boat's rudder to greatest effect.

For the longest time they seemed to make little progress as the mist around them thickened to shield whatever lay beyond.

Then, gradually, shapes became identifiable. A tiny island with a few trees dotting its landscape slipped past. For a few minutes the rain eased and Callie picked out a shoreline, a huge promontory, and—rocks!

"If it gets stormier, we're going to be smashed up against those." She knew he'd already considered it, but she couldn't just remain silent. They were in this position because of her, because she had to take one more job.

For the first time since she'd begun working for Finders Inc. Callie wished she'd quit long before Iraq had happened. In her heart, she knew her spirit had changed after that mission. She knew why—because she was afraid to face the possibility that maybe she'd lost her edge, lost the one asset that had made her valuable to the company. Her ability to fade into the woodwork, to become whomever she needed to be to get the job done was no longer the simple matter it had once been. Especially with Max nearby.

Living a lie had cost them both too much.

"Don't worry. We're going to be just fine." But Max's face tightened into harsh lines as he forced the controls to respond.

Callie sat silent. But she couldn't make herself stop thinking about what her life had become since those few hours in that war-torn country. That's where she'd lost her identity.

"Now we wait." With the anchor down, Max switched off the cruiser's running lights and all his instruments. Outside the wind howled, the waves tossed them back and forth, rain spattered the glass of the cabin. Inside there was only a faint glow from a small security light at the base of the instrument panel.

"For how long?" she whispered as the wind hissed in between the cracks as if to remind her that they were alone out here, at the mercy of the elements and whoever was following them.

"We'll wait as long as it takes. Are you afraid?" Max's arm slid around her waist, his voice quiet, confident. "We're safe, Cal. As long as he doesn't run into us, we'll be fine."

"Maybe he has GPS, too." She surprised herself by her willingness to snuggle her face against Max's sweater and let him decide what needed to be done.

Maybe it was the throbbing in her shoulder that the painkillers couldn't quiet. Maybe it was the ever-present knowledge that she'd messed up—again. Whatever the excuse, she didn't move away, didn't deny herself the pleasure of knowing that for once she didn't have to be strong and in control.

For now she'd do whatever Max told her.

"Doesn't matter if he does." His breath whispered across the tip of her ear. "Your hands are freezing. Come on, stand up. I'll warm you up." His arm urged her out of the chair until she was standing before him, wrapped in his arms, facing the storm in front of them.

Callie didn't have the strength or the desire to protest. Fortunately Max took her silence for fear.

"You're safe, babe. With nothing running we look like another rock sticking out of the ocean and he's not looking for a rock." He chuckled. "Besides, we've got God on our side."

Like that would make a difference.

Callie wanted to scoff at his confidence but she couldn't. God was important to Max, probably the most important thing in his life. Let him believe if he wanted to. Maybe God would reward faith as strong as his.

"There was a hymn my grandmother used to sing to me. When I was a kid I always hated lightning and she'd rock me and sing until I wasn't afraid anymore. One line of that song has stayed with me for years. 'He hideth my soul in the cleft of the rock and covers me there with his hand.' That's what this seems like—as if God is hiding us here. Don't you think?"

Like she was hiding in Max's arms? Callie bit her lip. Truth time.

"I've never really thought of God the way you do, Max, as if He's right here beside me."

"Why not?"

"Because—well, He's God. I'm just me."

"And?" He rested his chin on top of her head. His voice rumbled down, soft, gentle. "We're God's children, Cal. He cares about us, wants us to depend on Him, to come to him. That's why He created us—"

The pain in her heart exploded. "God isn't human."

"No, He's not. But He is love. Can you imagine overflowing, boundless love with no way to express it?" His hands found hers, fingers meshing. "God created us to love us. He knows us so well, he knows how many hairs we have on our head. He saw us before we were born, knew how we'd look, what we'd do. He's our father."

Callie pulled away from the shelter of his arms.

"Don't," she begged. "Please don't."

"You can't stuff it away forever." Tenderness filled Max's voice. "We had a baby, honey. He's not here anymore, but that doesn't mean God didn't see him, didn't know what his future held."

"Then why didn't He stop it?" she screamed. In fury she seized the edges of his jacket and held on. "If God is so loving, why didn't He save my innocent child?"

The flash of lightening illuminated his face highlighting stark, raw pain.

"I don't know," he whispered. "Maybe—"

"Maybe what? Maybe if you'd known you could have done something? Maybe if I hadn't gone? Maybe if I'd been more careful? Is that what you mean?" Callie felt tears dripping down her cheeks and dashed them away. "Hindsight is easy. But your God knew beforehand and He let it happen. How can you believe in God if He lets babies die to pay for their mothers' mistakes, Max?"

"Callie, that isn't—"

A loud thump cut off his words. He pressed a finger to her lips then peered into the inky darkness. She knew he was waiting for a flash of lightning, hoping desperately for a glimpse that would tell them who or what was outside.

Callie scoured the shadows with him, wondering how she could have imagined she was ready for this assignment. Her body ached, she was desperately tired.

But more than that, her soul felt empty, abandoned, as if life had ceased to matter.

What lurked outside mattered for Max's sake, because she didn't want him to pay for her folly. Only now did Callie fully accept how stupid she'd been to have allowed him to come, to let him leave Ketchikan with her.

She eased out of his arms, bent down, lifted her pant leg and felt the smooth, cool chill of gunmetal against her palm. Protection—but would it be enough?

She wrapped her fingers around the doorknob.

"Stay here, Max. Don't move out of this cabin. I don't want to shoot you by accident."

"You can't go out there, Cal! It's pouring, it's dark. You'll never see—"

"You have so much faith in your God, Max. Why don't you try putting a little in me?" Anger burst like fireworks inside, stinging deeply at his utter lack of confidence in her abilities. She spared a moment to settle her nerves, then drew in a deep breath. "Stay here."

She opened the door and stepped into the storm. At first Callie could see nothing through the impenetrable darkness that surrounded them. The wind slashed rain across her face and she had to pull her cap down to shield her eyes. Gradually her retinas adjusted to the shadows and objects became identifiable.

A blob of black loomed in the distance until lightning illuminated an outcropping of rocks in a heap where it had broken away from the cliff and tumbled down to the shore. Closer, just to the left, she glimpsed the ghostly outline of shoals, dangerous, murky—not fifty feet from the boat's fragile hull. Max had steered perilously close.

Knowing the danger did not come from shore, Callie

edged her way around to the other side of the boat, glad that her rain jacket was a deep navy and wouldn't give away her presence if anyone was watching from the open water. The wind, the combination of splashing water and pouring rain made it difficult to see.

She crouched against the front of the wheelhouse using the cover of the mainsail to scan the turbulent seas as she searched for something—anything that would explain the noise they'd heard.

Time crawled by, or perhaps it raced. Callie had no sense of how long she waited. She only knew something lay out there, waiting.

She was thoroughly soaked and freezing when she heard the soft pad of footsteps on the wooden deck. Max. He found her soundlessly, crouched down beside her without saying a word. Together they waited. Eventually the rain eased off leaving behind a thick misty fog that shrouded everything in a blanket of obscurity.

"Callie—"

His whisper died as a new sound echoed over the water. *Slap. Slap. Slap.*

"Paddles." Max's lips pressed against her ear. "Someone's rowing."

She nodded to show she understood, but said nothing, ears attuned to each nuance that floated toward them.

"I can't see a thing. You might as well admit we lost them. We'll be lucky if we don't get lost ourselves in this pea soup."

Though the voice was soft-spoken, with the storm now silent Callie clearly heard every word. She rested a hand on Max's arm, hoping he understood her caution to stay where he was.

"Shut up!" The hissed retort from an unknown voice sounded inches away yet Callie saw nothing.

A loud thud reverberated.

"What was that?"

"We ran into a rock."

"Now will you admit this is hopeless? We'll have to go back, wait for daylight." The wheedling voice died away as the slap of paddles grew fainter in the night until they could hear nothing. Sometime after that the sound of an engine broke the eerie quiet. It chugged away from them.

Then silence.

Callie rose, stretched to ease the kinks from her body. The fog was not lifting. They would be safe until morning.

"Did you recognize who that was?"

She shook her head, then realized that he couldn't see her. "No. Neither of the voices sounded familiar."

"Let's go below, get out of these damp clothes."

"I'm going to hang around up here for a while. Just to make sure." She moved into the cabin, shed her sopping jacket. "Don't turn on any lights," she warned as his hand reached out toward the dash.

"I wasn't going to." Max hung his own jacket on one of the brass hooks then reached down to flick a switch. Immediately a soft yellow glow sent a warm blast of air into the room.

"Don't worry, the batteries are topped up. I checked before we left. We can leave it running for a while with no problem."

"Good."

The heating coils cast just enough of a glow that she could read his expression, then she realized the reverse was also true. Not yet ready to let him see how worried she was, Callie replaced her gun, eased onto one of the stools. "I can't believe they were so close and still missed us."

"I can." He grinned. He sat down beside her. "It's exactly what I prayed for. God hears, Callie. Always."

"Yeah. Sure." She refused to go there again. "Hey, if it wasn't those two, then what was that noise we heard earlier?"

"I don't know." Max frowned at the reminder. "Maybe we bumped a piece of driftwood."

"Or maybe we hit something. You're pretty close to an outcropping."

"Didn't sound like that." He slid off his stool, put his jacket back on. "I'm going to take another look."

"But what if—" She didn't want to say it, but the image of someone hurting Max refused to leave her mind. Callie swallowed. "Be careful," she murmured.

His hand cupped her chin, holding her face so she couldn't avoid his penetrating stare.

"You worry about me too much, Cal. If someone's out there, waiting, then I'll deal with it. But I won't stay locked up in here, afraid to find the truth because I'm too scared to face it." His thumb brushed the corner of her mouth. "I trust God. Nothing happens that He doesn't allow. So I'm actually quite safe because I'm in His hands."

Callie didn't know how to answer that. Silence gaped between them as she stared into his eyes. What she saw there made her heart pick up speed, but she wasn't prepared when his head ducked down and he brushed his lips against hers.

His kiss shocked her with its gentleness. And yet it was intense, too. A thousand emotions swam though her body as his hand slipped down to the back of her neck and urged her closer. When he finally pulled back she found herself both sad it had ended and glad to be free of his encompassing presence. When Max was around her brain scrambled.

"Why did you do that?" she whispered, touching her bottom lip with one finger in bemusement.

"Because I needed to," he said simply. Then he turned and left.

The sound of the door closing behind him jerked her back to awareness. Callie scrambled to draw her reserves around her, to stop herself from wanting more. But it was harder now, especially because she knew she loved him as much as she ever had.

And because she knew a marriage based on a lie was hopeless.

So she would finish this job. But once it was complete she would never see Max again. That's the way it had to be.

A noise outside chased away her thoughts. She slipped her arms into her jacket sleeves and hurried outside, pausing just long enough to find the source of the sound.

Finally she spotted Max's kneeling figure outlined on the bow. He moved a long pole in the water, back and forth, as if trying to catch something. She watched him for several moments, eyes alert in case someone else appeared. But they were alone. Callie moved toward him.

"Fishing?" she whispered, crouching beside him, trying to get a look into the dark water below.

"You could say that." He scooped something into the net at the end of his pole and rose. "Finally."

Callie stepped backward as he suspended the net over the deck and reached to grasp the object inside.

"There's your thunk," he said, holding up a bottle. "My guess is this was tossed around by the storm. We just happened to be in the wrong place and bumped into it. Hence the thunk."

"I'm not so sure." She stepped forward, picked up the bottle with two fingers and sniffed the opening at the top. "This had gas in it and there's something stuffed inside. I'd say it was meant to be a Molotov cocktail. I'd like to get a closer look."

"Let's go inside." Max followed her to the cabin, switched on the lights.

"Are you sure that's safe?" Callie set the bottle on the dash for a better look.

"This fog is too thick for anyone to see our meager lights unless they're alongside," he answered. "I'm pretty certain our visitors won't be back tonight." He watched her study the bottle. "Well?"

"It hasn't been in the water that long. The label's barely loose. Also there's nothing growing on it as I'd expect if it had been floating around for a while." She twisted and turned the bottle, using a handkerchief just in case she ever had a chance to get it to Finders to look for prints. "Off the top, that's about all I can tell."

"Well, in the absence of more information, I think we have to assume that it floated near us."

A whirring sound had them both checking out the media console. The fax machine lit up and paper began to spew from it. Callie walked over to it, waiting impatiently for the printing to end, then picked up the sheet.

"It's from Finders," she told him. She scanned the page, held it out for Max to read. "*Windchaser* is owned by Josiah Harpnell's stepson, Aaron Eade."

Max read the information, frowned. "Stepson. Does he have a claim on Josiah?"

"I was told not."

"For a man who has no claim he's going to a lot of work to follow us."

"If it was him," Callie reminded. "We don't know that for sure."

"Then maybe it's time we did." Max turned the paper over, laid it on the console and handed her a pen. "Let's ask Daniel to fax us a picture of this guy. If we encounter him again, I'd like to know what he looks like."

Callie scribbled the note quickly and sent it. When she turned around she caught Max staring at the bottle, his mouth tight. He looked up and she knew exactly what he was thinking. She glanced down at the white sheet in her hands as a prickle of awareness crawled up her spine.

Subject is known to favor red plaid in his clothing. His maternal grandfather was Robert McEwen, owner of the McEwen Mills in Scotland. Current location: Los Angeles or Juneau. Info not clear.

Callie tracked Max's gaze to the bottle. Inside on the bottom lay a bright square of red plaid. Aaron Eade wasn't in Juneau. He was sailing the Inside Passage.

Somebody's information was very wrong.

SIX

Max thrust his face into the wind, relishing the velvet rush of sea air and sun on his face as he steered through the sea corridor he loved. Earlier he'd opened up two of the helm windows to allow fresh air in.

Despite the fact that the temperature outside hadn't yet risen appreciably, he breathed in deeply, enjoying the crisp coolness that chased away those negative thoughts waiting to crowd his mind.

This is the day the Lord has made.

Not a sound marred the glory of the morning—if you ignored the occasional squawk of a hungry seagull and the creak of the rigging overhead. The binoculars offered occasional glimpses of a hunting camp almost buried in the forest, or small villages dotting the coastline and interspersed throughout the bays and islands they passed. Their sails carried them soundlessly north, toward the place he'd have to leave Callie.

Max hadn't wakened her. One peek into her cabin had assured him that she was sound asleep, probably thanks to one of those pills. She needed the rest. Her face was pale. Shadows under her eyes added to the gaunt look of her cheeks. He'd felt a twinge of remorse that he hadn't been there to smooth her path, ease whatever had caused them.

Callie was hiding something.

He'd known it yesterday. Maybe, he admitted, he'd even known earlier and chosen to ignore it. But the past was done. He couldn't go back, only forward. The question was what to do about the future—and that divorce.

Overhead a float plane banked for descent somewhere behind the ridge of cedars that protected the coast.

Freedom. That's what he and Callie needed. Freedom from the pain, the mistakes, the sad memories. Freedom to seek out a new future—together. If only she'd try.

The bottle he'd fished out last night was tucked safely into a wall hook. A cold chill chased up his spine at the memory of Callie's face as she'd examined it. He'd seen that look before. She was steeling herself for something.

"Good morning."

He turned, spotted her standing in the doorway, curls running riot over her head. Her T-shirt and jeans were rumpled. Except for that sweater yesterday, she hadn't worn the clothes he'd had Shelby order.

"Good morning yourself. Did you sleep well?"

"Yes, thank you." So polite. As if they were strangers. "How long have we been under way?"

"About an hour." Max indicated their approximate position on a nearby map. "We're here."

"See anything interesting yet?"

Her words coincided with his sighting of something offshore about half a mile in front of them. He picked up the binoculars.

"Maybe." He honed in on the dot. "Well, fancy meeting you here."

"What?"

"Our friends in *Windchaser* are sitting in that inlet over there. Can't see anyone moving so I'm guessing they're still asleep."

Callie accepted the binoculars from him, found the spot and studied the boat. "They must have kept moving last night after they left us. Isn't that dangerous?"

"It can be. But the fog would have lingered closer to shore. If they headed out to deeper water and stayed there, there's a chance they could have found clearer sailing. Anyway, I'm sure they've got all the latest instruments to guide them judging by her exterior. If my guess is right, she's only a year or so old."

"Won't they follow us now?"

"Only if they see us." Max smiled at her worried tone. "Relax, Cal. It's five-thirty and we're running under sail so we shouldn't wake anyone up. With a bit of luck we'll glide on past and *Windchaser* and her crew will be none the wiser." He hoped. "There's a fax for you."

He pointed to the paper still lying in the machine.

Callie lifted it out studied the face he'd already scrutinized. "Josiah's stepson," she murmured. "He doesn't look like someone who'd chase me."

"Maybe he didn't. Maybe someone else is." He decided to broach a new subject, see how she'd respond. "Callie, why did you go to Iraq?"

Her whole body froze. Only her head turned. Her empty eyes stared at him.

"Why are you asking?"

"Because I need to know." Max had a thousand things he wanted to say but he shoved them away to concentrate on the most pertinent. "I've wanted to know for a long time but you weren't around to ask."

"I delivered some papers."

"You *had* to take the assignment?" That sounded like criticism and Max hadn't meant it to be. He'd have to make her understand that. "I mean—"

"I know what you mean. I didn't *have* to, I suppose Shelby could have sent someone else. But I had the doctor's clearance, I was only midway in the pregnancy with no complications. There was nothing dangerous about the mission."

Nothing dangerous? In Iraq? It was a war zone!

"There seemed no reason to refuse."

The words hung out there, so utterly untrue—as they both now knew.

"Can you tell me what happened?"

"No." She turned away.

"Please?" His fingers clenched on the controls but Max kept his voice steady. "I promise I won't harangue you or blame you, but I need to know what happened. I don't understand why I wasn't called when you were hurt. You're my wife." He clenched his teeth together at the spear of pain that ached inside. "It was my baby, too."

Callie studied him for a moment before she slumped onto a stool. Her thin shoulders lifted as she pulled a deep breath into her lungs. She stared straight through the windshield.

"I suppose I owe you that much." The dead calm of her voice scared him with its lack of emotion.

"It's not about owing anything, Callie. I just want to know. For my own peace of mind. I've asked myself a thousand times if there was something I could have done if I'd been there. Some way I could have made a difference. For weeks I'd lie awake at night imagining that if I'd had a chance—"

"It wasn't like that, Max. Nothing you could have done would have prevented it." Her blue eyes flashed with sparks of temper. "You want to know? Fine. I'll tell you. Then I don't want to talk about it again."

The sparks died. Her voice dropped almost to a whisper. Her gaze remained on the ocean in front of them.

"I was riding in a jeep. A sniper took a shot that blew out a tire. The driver couldn't handle it and we rolled. I was thrown from the vehicle. By the time they got me to the hospital it was too late." She shoved her knuckles against her mouth, forced herself to regain control.

Then she straightened, faced him, whispered, "The baby had already died."

"But if someone had called, I could have—"

"There was nothing anyone could do, Max. It was too late."

I could have been there with you. I could have held you. We could have shared it together. His hands clenched at his sides as he stemmed the words.

"I guess my bag must have been thrown quite some distance because it took them a couple of days to find it and my ID. By the time they did I was well enough to leave on my own. I came ho—back."

Max knew she'd meant to say "home." Only she hadn't come home. At least not for long. She'd broken the news in a cold, hard little voice then said she needed to be alone for a while. He'd let her go because he was afraid not to, afraid she'd crack and break and he'd never see her again. Next thing he knew she had headed to Australia.

"It must have been horrible," he murmured, trying to understand. "I wish I'd been there for you."

"It wouldn't have done any good."

He let that go, remained silent until he was certain she'd regained her composure. Then he asked the question that had chewed at his soul ever since he'd been served those papers.

"Our baby dying—is that why you want the divorce?"

"Yes. Mostly." She slid off the stool, zipped her jacket the rest of the way and thrust her hands into her pockets.

"I've seen what losing a child can do to a marriage that isn't already rock solid. We both know ours was never that." Callie held his gaze, forcing him to see the truth written all over her face. "For a little while I let myself believe you were right, that a family would make it better. I shouldn't have done that. Not when I knew the truth."

"What truth?"

"I don't want to be a mother. Not ever. And that's why we can't be married anymore, Max."

He could find nothing to say to stop her when she turned, walked out of the cabin and disappeared down below.

Callie hadn't wanted their baby? He could hardly tolerate the thought. But after a few moments of reflection he knew that wasn't true. She'd always seemed drawn to kids. When Shelby's daughter had been kidnapped, Callie had spent hours of her own time tracking down leads, desperate to rescue the little girl.

He remembered a Christmas party they'd once attended. Callie had disappeared partway through the evening. He'd assumed she was talking to their hostess in another room until it was time to leave and she wasn't with the others. He'd found her in the kids' playroom, one little boy on her lap, another by her side listening raptly as she'd read the entire group a story about the Littlest Angel. When she was finished, she'd kissed each cheek with a tenderness he'd seldom seen and when they got home she'd disappeared into her workroom in the basement where she'd sewn a stuffed toy for each of them.

No, Callie had wanted their child. Max was sure of it. She mourned the loss of that tiny life deeply, he'd seen that for himself.

Was it because of the anguish she'd suffered, still suffered, that she'd turned her back on motherhood? Or was it something else?

Max checked his position. *Windchaser* was now well behind them and apparently not catching up. He could pull in somewhere, go below and talk to her. He decided to wait.

Tracy Arm wasn't that far away. Given the speed they were moving now, they should be able to drop anchor some time this afternoon. Then he'd find out what was going on inside her head and figure out how to deal with it.

Shame washed over him.

"I haven't done that often enough, have I, Lord?" He'd never even guessed she felt this way. Callie had talked so little about her childhood, but that was his fault. He'd been so intent on pursuing their future, he'd assumed the past didn't matter.

That speech about her father made it obvious he'd been wrong.

* * *

"This place is fantastic." Callie leaned back on the chaise, trying to absorb the view. Giant icebergs towered above her in three directions. "Why are some of the layers such a rich blue?"

"It's glacial ice water that's been compacted really tightly from the weight of all that ice. Look over there!" Max's arm brushed hers as he pointed in front of them. "Watch and listen."

A sound pierced the silence of the bay.

"That's called white thunder." He grinned. "There's more so keep listening."

Moments later frosted chips snapped off and flew through the air as the monstrous mountain of ice in front of them fractured. After more rumbling one piece sheared completely away from the ancient glacier and dropped into the mirror surface of the bay, sending up a spray of icy water as the jagged gleaming point sank then bobbed above the water. The bay echoed with a sibilant hiss.

"Ice sizzle," Max told her. "It happens when thousands of air bubbles are released from glacial ice."

"It's unbelievable. And so massive."

"That's why it's better to stay back here, why I didn't want to get too close. The calves can sink you in their backwash, never mind running aground on what lies beneath the water."

"Calves?"

"That's what they call the pieces that break off. These icebergs are calving. It's really something when you think about how long ago this iceberg was formed, how long it's been around. This ice is approximately 10,000 years old."

"How come there's no one else here watching?"

Max shrugged.

"It's late in the cruise season but the ships are still doing the route. Maybe they've already been here today. I imagine they'll be back tomorrow or the next day."

"This day is perfect." Callie snuggled into her deck chair, glad of the feather quilt Max had brought up. The air felt cooler here, the breeze off the icebergs frigid with only a light jacket for protection. And yet the sun's rays heated her cheeks.

Her phone rang.

"Hi, Lisa." A bubble of delight formed inside her heart at the sound of that smart-aleck voice. "What's up?"

Callie's joy drained away as Lisa spoke. A sense of dread took its place.

"I might know him. I'm not sure. He could be part of a case I'm working on. Are you all right?"

Anger filled her as Lisa described her injuries.

"I'm so sorry he did that. You go to the doctor and make sure everything's healing properly. No, don't put me off. You need to get checked out in case something's really wrong. Then head over to my place. You know where the key is. You can hide out there for a while."

Callie hung up, fully aware that Max had heard every word.

"Who was that?"

"A friend of mine in Victoria, a teenage runaway. Lisa goes to a teen center where I've been helping out. She's been trying to get off the street. A couple of days ago she wanted to see me. She left a message. We usually meet at a burger joint near my place. Lisa's always hungry." She smiled at the memory. "When I didn't show, she got worried. She was on her way to Finders to find out where I was when some guy grabbed her. When she couldn't tell him where I was he started beating on her. It happened the day we left."

"Is she all right?"

"Bruised, nothing broken, she says. Black eye, swollen lip. She's survived worse, believe me, but not usually because of me."

"Any idea who the creep is?"

"From her description I'd guess he's our friend, Josiah's stepson."

"He knows enough about you to tackle a girl you've been working with?" Max's mouth tightened. "This is sounding worse by the minute. The guy knows too much. He seems determined to get to you."

"Yes, but why?" Callie couldn't make the pieces fit. "He has no legal standing; he's not Josiah's heir. He has no reason to expect to inherit. We've never met. So why come after me? There is no other connection between us."

"As far as you know." The grim tones gave away his anger.

"This pursuit—if it's Aaron it doesn't make sense." She began to lay out what she knew. "I'm sure I read a report at Finders that Aaron Eade was reported in L.A. The fax that came in said L.A. or Juneau. If he was in either he we would have had to fly into Victoria, have transport ready and someone in place who could tell him where I was— and when—in order to follow us from Ketchikan. That's not including the little side trip to beat up Lisa."

"Maybe he's working with someone." Max tilted his face into the sun.

"Maybe." Callie told herself to stop staring. She

pulled out the sheet of paper with Aaron's face on it, studied the information below. "There's nothing here to indicate he's ever had any brushes with the law. Who would he recruit?"

"All I know is that's not the guy who was watching you in Ketchikan. Could be your Mr. Eade recruited someone to help him?" Max scratched his chin.

"Who? And why?"

"A museum wants the artifacts, maybe. They know that Josiah won't give them away, but if he wasn't there, somebody else would be put in charge to deal with the estate—maybe even help them."

"Okay, that implicates the museum. But how does that involve Aaron Eade? What's in it for him?"

"I have no idea. Is it something Finders could investigate?"

"They could—if they had something to go on. We don't have much." Callie thought for a minute, then began dialing. "I'll ask Shelby to dig up everything they can on the people who would handle the estate if Josiah wasn't there, and to get me more info on Aaron. Maybe by tomorrow we'll get a clue as to why he would follow me. If he is."

She made the call fully aware that the twitching muscle at the corner of Max's mouth expressed his irritation better than any words he could utter. He didn't like not knowing what was ahead, he never had. That's why she'd never discussed her missions with him.

Callie finished her call, tucked her phone into her pocket.

"So?"

"They'll get back to me."

"Right." His fists curled against his thigh.

"Look, I know it's frustrating, Max. But sometimes that's how we have to work. Nobody ever knows all there is to know about a situation before they go into it."

"I can't help thinking you should have known a lot more about this."

"Finders Inc. was given the case at the last minute. It's not surprising they don't have all the details nailed down."

"And your trip to Iraq? Was that at the last minute, too?"

Callie froze. "As a matter of fact it was."

"That didn't turn out very well, either, did it?" His eyes hardened. "Maybe you like tackling the unknown."

Callie caught her breath.

"Are you accusing me of something, Max?"

"No. But don't you think it's unusual that you seem to gravitate toward these cases? Iraq, the Outback, Alaska. I can't help wondering if you choose them because of the danger."

"Do you have any idea how insulting that is?" She rose to stand in front of him. "If you want to blame me for the baby's death, go ahead. Finders isn't at fault."

"Who is?"

His white face stared back at her, the pain in his eyes unshielded and heart-wrenching. In that moment Callie wanted to gather him to her, to whisper promises that she'd make it up to him, that she'd help him forget, that they'd move past the pain to something new, something better.

But that wasn't true and she knew it. Some things couldn't be forgotten. Some pain just had to be endured.

"I'm to blame, Max. Me and God—the one you think

is so loving." She stared into the sky, let the anger wash away the pain. "Ask Him why He let it happen."

"Do you think I haven't?"

At first Callie wasn't certain she'd heard him correctly. The admission had cost Max dearly. He was hurting as much as she was.

"I've asked, Callie. I prayed. But the baby's still dead." His head lifted. He looked her straight in the eye. "And now you're leaving, too."

"I have to. We don't belong together, Max. Maybe we never did." She thrust back her shoulders, forced out the words. "I've changed. I'm not who you need. To pretend means living a lie and I refuse to do that anymore."

Except for one lie that she would never admit to.

He rose, moved to stand in front of her. "Who are you, Callie?"

"What?"

"You said you've changed. Who are you now? What's different?" He tilted his head to one side, waited for her answer.

"It's not something that can be quantified—like the ratio of speed to engine power." She shifted, feeling pinned down, confined.

"What is it then? I really want to know."

A bubble of anger burst at his unblinking stare. "Stop it."

"I can't. What's changed, Callie?"

She drew in a breath of courage, let out a burst of truth.

"Everything. I'm a loner. I always have been. I don't like big, noisy crowds with people scrutinizing my every move. I like to fade into the woodwork, observe without being observed."

"That's not new." Still his gaze held hers. "What's changed, Callie?"

The pressure of that steady regard was getting to her. Callie scoured the glistening icebergs as if they held the answers she needed. She found no help.

"I don't believe in God."

"Same old, same old." A funny little grin tugged at his lips. "Try again, Cal."

"I don't like people pressing me," she blurted out, surprised when he laughed.

"Like now? You never did before, either. Tell me what's new about that."

Her patience thinned. If he kept pushing she was going to tell him a lot more than he wanted to hear. Callie glared at him.

"I'm not a sweet, quiet woman who wants to spend her days waiting for her husband to notice her. I don't want to be a hausfrau, I have no desire to spend my life on committees or waste my time having coffee with the girls."

"Who asked you to?"

"What?" Callie blinked, surprised by that. "You don't want a wife?"

"Oh, I want a wife, all right. My wife. But I couldn't care less if you clean the house yourself, hire somebody to do it, or leave it for me. Now tell the truth. What about you has changed?"

"I don't want you to spend any time at some condo in the city when we have a perfectly good home." The old grudge that had burned like acid in her soul burst out of her.

"Since I don't work in the city I don't need it anymore anyway. So we'll sell it. What else?"

Had she just agreed to live with him again? Callie frowned. This wasn't going at all as she'd planned.

"I'm not some innocent little girl you have to protect, Max. I'm strong, I'm capable and I know how to take care of myself. I don't need or want anyone to second-guess my decisions."

"Fine. You can duke it out when we meet up with this Eade fellow. I'll sit back and watch."

"You're not taking me seriously."

"Sure I am, Cal." Max leaned against the railing and studied her. But since he slid on his sunglasses she couldn't see what he was thinking. "I've heard every word you've said. But you're talking about the past and I want to hear what's different now."

"Everything."

"Like?"

Ooh, he was so frustrating. Callie turned her back, stared at the ice monoliths in front of her and wondered what he'd do if he heard the truth. Like she didn't know that he'd walk away. For good.

"I'm just—different. There are things in my past that you don't know about, Max. Things that would change the way you think of me. I never told you because I don't want to talk about them and because I think they're better left buried."

His arm slid around her shoulder, drew her against his side.

"I disagree. If the past is bothering you then it's obvious you need to talk about it."

"I can't."

He reached up and touched her chin, coaxing her to look at him. His voice softened, his eyes caressed her.

"You're not going to change how I think of you, you know. It doesn't matter what dark secrets you've buried. I made a promise to love you until death parts us and I'm sticking to my side of the bargain, Callie Merton Chambers."

How could she argue with that?

As she struggled to find the answers she needed, Callie realized Max was going to kiss her. Half of her wanted—no—*craved* his touch. The other half screamed a warning that giving in would only bring more pain in the long run. But wouldn't it be worth it?

Callie gave in.

Max had always been gentle, infinitely tender. This time was no different. He brushed his lips against her forehead, touched each eyelid, feather-dusted the tip of her nose. Then he stopped.

Callie opened her eyes to see why.

He was watching her, his eyes brimming with something she'd thought she'd lost forever.

"I love you, Callie. I don't care about your past. I want your future."

His lips moved over hers, demanding a response she couldn't deny. Her arms lifted, curled around his neck, drawing him nearer, close enough to hear the longing of her heart.

She kissed him back knowing he would read more into her response than she wanted, but desperate to once again experience the joy she'd always found in his arms.

A long time later he lifted his head, searched her face. "Callie—"

She touched a fingertip to his lips, shook her head.

"Not now," she whispered. "Please, not now."

Finally he nodded. She turned, his arms still holding her, and gazed across the water at the beauty surrounding them. Max's chin grazed her hair as he bent and brushed his lips against her ear.

"Not now," he agreed. "But soon. You can't keep hiding, Callie. Whatever it is, I'll understand. Just don't keep secrets from me."

But she had to.

Otherwise her marriage would surely die.

So she stood, quietly content to watch the icebergs calve off chunks of ten-thousand-year-old ice, freeing them to float in the water alone.

"God's in His Heaven, all's right with the world," Max murmured.

It didn't seem that way to Callie.

The peal of the fax machine erupted into their peaceful afternoon. Max sighed, slid his hands down her arms then drew away.

"I'll get it." He strode across the deck, climbed into the captain's cabin. A moment later his head reappeared. "Callie, you'd better take a look at this."

The peace that moments ago had soothed her soul, jettisoned overboard as Callie walked forward.

One glance at Max told her the news wasn't good.

She took the paper, read the notification from Finders.

Aaron Eade had arrived in Victoria by commercial flight from Los Angeles *after* the assault on Lisa had occurred.

Someone else was pursuing her.

SEVEN

Max weighed anchor six miles from Juneau Harbor. From all reports the city was still socked in with fog. Rather than berth near someone they didn't know he elected to anchor in a little cove, spend the night and head into port in the morning.

He'd tell Callie so, if she ever came up top.

According to his watch she'd been below a long time, ever since they'd left Tracy Arm—after she'd read the fax from Finders. Max knew why. She was weighing options, devising a plan and bottling up her worries. He wished she'd open up, share her fears, let him in.

Why hadn't he ever asked her to?

The question came from out of the blue—but it stunned him into realizing he'd never really encouraged Callie to talk about her missions. Maybe she'd taken that as disinterest.

A noise from below alerted him to her ascent.

"Are you hungry?" Callie emerged looking as if she'd just stepped out of the shower. Her hair, frizzy with drying curls, drooped almost to her shoulders. She wore no makeup, but had pulled on fresh clothes. "I made a meal."

"I'm starving." With everything secured, Max climbed down from the captain's cabin and sniffed. "Smells great. Do you want to eat up here so we can watch the sunset?"

"Okay." She disappeared for a moment then carried a tray up the steps. "If you'll take this, I'll get the rest."

Silence reigned for the few moments it took to get the table set and lay out the food.

"It looks great." He bowed his head, offered a short prayer of thanks, then picked up his fork. "You don't have to cook every meal," he told her. "I've gotten quite handy with eggs."

"Really?" Her fork stopped halfway to her mouth as she stared at him. "You never cooked before."

"It was time to learn then, wasn't it?" He shifted under her scrutiny. "I took a cooking class."

Callie choked. By the time she'd regained her composure Max wished he'd kept silent.

"It's not that big a deal. Lots of men learn how to cook."

"You never seemed interested before."

"I thought you didn't want me poking around in the kitchen. You said you hated the mess," he reminded.

"Did I?" Callie gave him a surprised look. "I don't remember that." After a moment she glanced down at her plate.

Max concentrated on his food, too, but his mind was busy with the past.

"I talked to Daniel again."

Something in her tone made his nerves kick into high alert. "And?"

"It seems Aaron Eade recently lost his job. He was clerking in the law firm that was supposed to handle

Josiah's estate. When he began asking too many questions, someone started investigating. Aaron Eade was fired."

"So maybe he blames his former stepdad for getting fired? Or maybe he was there for exactly that purpose. When did he finish?"

"Six weeks ago," Callie told him.

"How long have they been trying to contact Josiah?"

"That I don't know. The firm had no desire to admit their difficulties with the case. They did tell Shelby they'd hired an investigator who located Josiah but their location turned out to be wrong twice. Sound familiar?"

"Hmm."

"One of their people had an accident trying to get the papers delivered, too."

"A convenient accident."

"I was thinking the same thing. But it doesn't necessarily mean it's him. Eade's mother and Josiah have been divorced for years. Why would he try to get something after all this time?"

"Maybe he tried before and it didn't work." Max pushed away his plate, sipped the tea she'd poured. "None of this explains who the other guy is."

"What guy?"

"The one I saw watching you in Ketchikan. I'd feel better if we had something on him."

Callie seemed to fall into a stupor.

"What are you thinking?"

"Peter, my contact there, had a digital camera. He was snapping some shots before I walked up to him. Maybe he could e-mail them to Shelby so she could take a look, even pass them on to us. If you recognized a face, Finders could work on getting a name."

"It's an idea." He leaned back, listened as she made the call.

"Max thinks there's someone else involved, Shelby. I have no idea who. I don't know any of the primaries. Oh, I forgot to tell you about Lisa." Callie quickly relayed what she'd learned then clicked the phone closed. "Daniel's going to my place to talk to Lisa. They'll have her talk to a sketch artist—see what they come up with."

At least something was happening. Max supposed he should feel better about that. When Callie pushed back her chair, he stopped her.

"Let's just leave the dishes for now."

"Why?"

"Because you have to see an Alaskan sunset. Especially after a clear day like this. It's something you'll never forget." To forestall her objections he piled everything on the tray and carried it below. "I'll do them all later," he told her when he returned. "For now let's just relax."

She found it hard to sit there, he knew. Callie had nervous energy to burn. Maybe that's why she'd chosen Finders in the first place.

"What will you do after this assignment?" he asked, curious about her long-term thoughts.

"Take the next one, probably." She spread a blanket over the chaise, sank into it, then wrapped it around herself.

"Is that all you want?"

"I don't know what you mean," she said. "Finders Inc. is my employer. I go where they send me. You know that."

"Yeah, I do. But is that it? Year after year you'll go traipsing around the world?"

"Not necessarily." A defensive note entered her voice. Her eyes hardened. "I suppose eventually I'll decide to stick closer to home, maybe take a job in the office. But I'm not there yet."

So how did he fit into that plan?

There had to be something left in their relationship. She couldn't have returned his kiss the way she had unless she still felt something for him. At least he prayed that was true. Maybe it was time to find out.

"What about me?" Max kept a bead on her, refused to look away.

"What about you?"

He shook his head. "You know what I'm asking, Callie. What's the future for us?"

"There is no 'us.' I told you that. It's over." She twisted slightly to stare at the mountains beyond.

"It's not over, Cal. Not by a long shot."

"You think that because I let you kiss me, because I kissed you back—that means we should stay married?" She shook her head, a wry grin tip-tilting her mouth in a sad smile. "I thought that was enough—once. But it isn't."

He straightened, intent on making her see he was serious about fixing whatever was wrong. "I love you, Callie. I can't just let you walk away without doing something. Talk to me."

"About what?"

He took a deep breath, then plunged in. "The baby?"

"No."

"We have to." He crouched down beside her chair, tilted her chin so he could see into her eyes, threaded his fingers through her cold ones. "That was our child. A special gift whose memory we should cherish. I want to know more."

Her lips pinched tightly together.

"Did you ever find out whether we had a boy or a girl?" He held his breath, praying desperately that she'd respond.

"A boy."

"I knew it." He grinned at her. "All that stuff about carrying high and not kicking you much—you were wrong."

Callie stared at him. "Max, he's dead," she whispered her voice cracking as she said the words.

"He's in Heaven—with God. My son is in Heaven." He closed his eyes as a rush of emotion filled him. "We had a son."

"Had. Remember that." She sounded hard, cold. But it was just a front, a facade to cover her true feelings.

"But he was ours. We created him together. That's a bond that can't be broken, Cal. Our child."

She stared at him. Something flickered to life in the depths of her eyes.

"He's buried in a graveyard about six miles out of Baghdad."

"Did you—?"

She shook her head.

"The doctor told me a nun who worked at the hospital arranged it. I had a stone made but I didn't know what name to put on it so I told them carve Baby Chambers on it." Her voice had dropped to a whisper. "One minute he was there with me. The next he was gone."

"Oh, Cal." He drew her off the chair and into his arms.

"It was like a horrible black dream, only I couldn't claw my way out of it." She wept, horrible wrenching sobs that told him she'd bottled her grief for too long. "I'm sorry I went, Max. I'm so sorry."

"Hush. You didn't do anything wrong," he whispered, pressing her face into his shoulder. "I know you didn't. It's just—life. We can't understand God's ways. We just have to get through it. We can do it together."

Her body tensed at that but she didn't pull away. Max kept talking, hoping she'd finally let go of the pain.

"We would have loved him, Cal. God knows that."

"Does He?"

"Of course. You love kids. I've seen you with them. You would have been the best mom in the world."

"I would have tried."

"I know." He brushed the fluff of curls away from her damp cheeks. "Did the accident stop you from delivering the letter or whatever you carried there?"

She jerked away from him, rose, smoothed her hands over her hair. Diamond-bright tears sparkled in her eyes but otherwise the mask was back in place.

"No. I did that first. I don't want to talk about it anymore."

"Can't you tell me what took you there in the first place?"

She shook her head, moved to sit on one of the benches at the side of the boat.

They still had a good half hour before the sun sank beneath the horizon. Max took himself below decks and made some hot chocolate while he ordered himself to calm down. She'd told him something and it was more than she'd been able to say for months. That was enough for tonight. Tomorrow he'd try again.

By the time he carried the mugs topside, the chill of the water around them was rapidly outweighing the sun's heat. He set the cup into her hands, sat down beside her to watch. Callie didn't seem to notice the coolness. She sat transfixed as three orca whales emerged a few hundred yards from their stern and began a spectacular show, dipping under the water and rising again in a magnificent display of power. They twisted and bobbed, ducked down and rose again numerous times, sometimes coming so near he feared they'd make a mistake and overturn the boat.

But they didn't. Gracefully they chose their splash zone, allowing their fantails to show as they plunged down. Then, all at once they disappeared into the deep and did not return. Seconds later the fax machine blared to life.

"You watch the sun," he murmured. "I'll get that."

Max climbed up to the helm, pulled out the paper, froze as his fingers curled around the edges.

"Callie? Can you come here? Now."

She appeared a moment later, her face still reflecting the wonder of what she'd just experienced. "What is it?"

"Finders sent us copies of Peter's photos. There's the man I saw." He pointed at the top corner of the sheet of photos. "He's the one who was watching you in Ketchikan."

She bent, peered at the picture.

"It's not very clear. Unless someone can enhance this, I don't think it's enough to go to police with. I certainly can't recognize anyth—" She caught her breath, leaned nearer as if something had caught her eye.

"What's wrong?"

"Nothing. The light hit the wrong way I guess." Her hand was shaking as she tucked the pages in a cubby hole. "I'll phone them. Maybe the lab can do enough work on the pictures to get the police going."

"Maybe." That wasn't all and Max knew it. He chose to let it go, pointed instead to the sinking sun. "There she goes."

Callie stood silent, watching as the big yellow orb sank behind snow-tipped mountains. "Lights out," she whispered.

"Not quite. There's a full moon tonight so we should be able to see quite well unless a squall blows up." He sensed a hesitation in her, as if she wasn't exactly sure of her next move—totally unlike Callie.

"I need to phone Finders."

"And I need to get those dishes washed off before we have to use a chisel. It was a great meal. Thank you."

"You're welcome." She sounded distant, her focus on her phone.

Max climbed down from the helm and moved below decks. She'd explain when she was ready. He hoped.

By the time he had everything safely stowed he still hadn't heard Callie's footsteps on the deck above. He grabbed a heavier jacket, went to find out why.

"I know they went to see you, Lisa. They'll send me a report about it eventually. But I need to know now. What did the guy who attacked you look like—exactly?" Callie sat huddled against the mast, her eyes tightly closed. "Anything you can tell me, please, Lisa."

It was like watching a turtle retreat. Callie nodded, murmured the right phrases, but her entire body seemed to flatten against the metal mechanism as she cringed at whatever the girl told her. After several minutes of very pointed questions she thanked Lisa then closed the phone. A soft trembling sigh eased out of her.

"Do you know him?"

Callie jerked around, blinked to rid her eyes of the moisture that had pooled there. "Who?"

"Whoever beat up your friend. Do you know who he is?"

"Not really. Lisa wasn't very clear." She rose, pushed her phone into her pocket. "The sea's like glass. I don't think there will be a storm tonight."

Trying to get him off the point. Anger bubbled up.

"Stop playing games and tell me what you know." He purposely stood directly in her path, waited for her response.

"I don't *know* anything." She glared at him. "I have some suspicions but that's all they are."

He raised one eyebrow.

"Stop it." Callie was furious. "You can't bully me into anything anymore, Max. I'm not a child to be quelled by that glare of yours, no matter how icy you make it."

He blinked. "Bully you?"

"It's your usual modus operandi. When I don't go along with your ideas, you try to push me into doing what you want."

"No, I don't."

"Yes, you do. You always have." She stepped around him, sat down on one of the bench seats. "Oh, you don't resort to twisting my arm, but you bully just the same."

She was deadly serious. Max sank into a chair, struggled to come to grips with the fact that his own wife felt like that. Was it true?

"How do I bully you, Callie?"

She gave him a hard look, judging his seriousness.

"I want to know. Really."

"You try coaxing first, wheedling. If that doesn't get

me to agree with you, you put up arguments about why
I can't do something. If I still don't fall in, you line everything up in mental columns and tick off one side
against the other, pros against the cons. Yours are always
the pros and they always outnumber mine."

He wanted to protest, to insist she was wrong, that
he wasn't like that. But he couldn't. Not with her looking
at him like that—as if she expected him to deny it.

"I don't think you mean to, but you do it, Max."

She kept looking at him, but never said a word. He
didn't blame her. Trust was hard to regain.

"I realize now that you had a lot of reservations
about being married, having a child, living the kind of
life I wanted. I never really helped you voice your
concerns or work them through and I should have.
That was my job as your husband." He took a deep
breath. "I apologize for ever making you feel anything
less than the most important person in my life. I guess
I got so wrapped up in my fairy-tale dream for us that
I never even considered you seriously didn't want
what I did."

"I thought I wanted children. Just not then." She slid
her hand from his, moved to a nearby seat. "I didn't have
a good childhood, Max. I told you that. I was lonely. I
wasn't the kind of kid who fit into my parents' social
life. I'm sure they were terribly embarrassed by my
tomboy ways."

It was the most she'd ever said about them. Max kept
silent, hoping she'd say more.

"As a teen I didn't have a lot of dates, I didn't go out
a lot. When I went to work for Finders Inc. I thought
my life would be full enough. And I was okay with that.

I didn't know there could be anything more, and maybe I was afraid to believe there would be."

She closed her eyes, leaned back.

"Then you came along. I never knew anyone like you, Max. You were so certain—about everything. I guess it was easier to let you make the decisions about our wedding, our home, our future. For a while, anyway."

"Until you began to resent it," he guessed.

"When it became painfully obvious that I had nothing in common with the rest of your life, I started to feel like I was your project, that you were trying to make me be like the rest of your life. Perfect. And I knew I couldn't be. I didn't fit."

"You fit just fine. I thought it would help if we had some friends in common. There was Daniel, of course. But you never seemed to have any women friends, other than people from work. I figured it would be nice for you to unwind if you had someone you could relax with, talk to." He held up his hands. "That's why I was always pushing you to go out with the group. It didn't mean I wanted you to be like them. I didn't want you to change at all. I loved—love you the way you are."

"It didn't seem like it," she whispered. "The first time I came back from a mission you had the living room furniture all moved around."

"So?" Max frowned. "I couldn't see the TV the way you had it before. Mary said—" He stopped, gulped.

"Yes." Callie nodded. "Mary said. And Andrea said we should cut down the weeping birch and put in a rose garden. Natalie said we should sign up at the country club. They all had a say in our life. Too much say."

"That isn't true!"

"Maybe it isn't. But that's what it felt like to me. The moment I said something—told you I didn't want to take up golf, that I wanted that birch tree and a swing under it, you brushed me off, tried to coax me to see how much better it would be to have a rose garden like Shelby's." She stared out over the water. "Every time I came back I felt a little less connected to you, a little less a part of your life."

"So you took longer missions, stayed away more." He raked a hand through his hair, frustrated by the futility of it all. "If you'd only said something—"

"I couldn't. I had to figure it out for myself first." The corners of her lips tilted in that self-mocking smile only Callie could produce.

"So where do we go from here?"

The smile disappeared. Tiny lines framed her eyes. "Nowhere."

"But—"

"It took me a long time to understand, but I know the truth now." She met his gaze, touched his cheek. "I can't be who you want, Max."

"I want you."

She shook her head, mahogany curls dancing in the moonlight. "You want someone you think I am. You have this fairy tale in your head and you're looking for happily ever after. But I'm not the princess in your story."

In other words there was nothing about the past she wanted to keep.

"What do you want?"

"I don't know for sure."

The starkness of it echoed through the soft lap of waves against the side of the boat.

"I just know I don't want to hurt you anymore."

"I'm a big boy, Cal. I can take it. I want to take it if it will help get our marriage back on track."

She rose in a rush of movement, turned on him like an angry cat.

"Haven't you been listening to anything I said? Our marriage is finished. It's over, Max."

He held her gaze, shook his head. "I don't accept that. The vows said 'till death do us part.' Until that happens I'll keep praying that God will heal us, give us hope for tomorrow."

"God again." She headed for the stairs, stopped on the first. "You'd do better to ask God to keep you safe. Who knows which nutcase will come after us tomorrow."

"He does." Max rose, watched her descend. "Good night, Callie."

She never answered. But that was okay. The person he really needed to hear from was upstairs.

Max grabbed the blanket she'd been using and wrapped himself in it. Then he tipped his face up to stare at the stars and talked to their creator.

Callie awakened suddenly, every nerve on high alert.

Something—a thud. What was it?

She listened, heard the muffle of steps overhead.

Someone was on the boat.

In seconds she had slipped out of bed, tugged on a sweater and was heading upstairs. She could see the stairs, which meant the cabin door hadn't been securely fastened.

Her racing heart died for a moment at the thought of Max lying facedown on deck. She forced back the fear, crept upward as she scoured the darkness for an intruder.

A hand slid over her mouth. She grabbed it to pull it away, realized it was Max. He moved slightly and she could see his face in the moonlight. He shook his head, beckoned.

Callie followed him on deck, stepping carefully behind him, avoiding the chairs that still sat where they'd left them. He led her to a shadowed spot to one side of the helm.

"Wait."

They stood together for several moments before she heard the noise again, saw the faint light wavering under the water. Tiny bubbles broke the skin of the ocean.

Someone was under their boat.

EIGHT

"Looks like the fog's completely dissipated in Juneau." Max expertly handled the craft so that the sails took them straight toward the marina. "If I can just get her docked now."

Callie clutched the edge of her seat as he manipulated their position through the other boats. Sailing into a full harbor was tricky and seldom done—too many opportunities to hit something. But they didn't dare use the motor. Max had donned a scuba suit and gone down at first light. Someone had damaged the prop. Without it, and not knowing what other havoc had been wreaked, they had only the sails to rely on.

She didn't know how long they'd stood on deck the night before, waiting. Time had no meaning as the night deepened and the intruder did his dirty work. Eventually Max insisted she go below and sleep while he kept watch. Callie had agreed—for three hours—then taken her turn on watch.

Sometime during that watch three other craft had dropped anchor near them. Callie watched them slide silently into place, saw the lights dim in each, kept vigil as they gently bobbed on the water. The next morning, one—*Harvest Rain*—agreed to follow them to Juneau. Just in case.

Now that they were here, all she wanted to do was get on with the case. After she made sure Max was safe. She picked up her phone and dialed Finders.

"We're in Juneau. The harbor is open. Everything's fine though we had someone tamper with the boat last night. Max is going to get it checked out. Where's the meet?" She pinched her lips together as Shelby informed her that her contact had not yet reported in.

"Josiah is known to change his mind at the drop of a hat. He may have done so again. We just don't know. With the fog, everything's been confused. It might be better if you and Max found something to do for a few hours while we try to verify what we've learned."

"Okay. I'll check back in after lunch." She slid the phone into her pocket as Max slid into the berth they'd phoned ahead for.

He managed it flawlessly, without marking the boat or the pier. His skill was amazing.

"So what now?" he asked once he'd tied off the boat.

"You find a mechanic or whatever you need. I'm going to scout around the town." She explained the Finders situation. "Maybe I can learn something if I poke around on my own."

"I don't think that's a good idea," Max murmured, his forehead furrowed. "Shelby said she'd check it out. Let her do her job. Besides, I have something I want to show you."

He wore that little boy look of eagerness that Callie had never been able to deny. At the same time she had a strange sensation of being watched. She turned slowly, scanned the area for someone she knew.

"Are you listening to me?"

"Not really." She honed in on one boat. Someone inside the helm had a pair of binoculars directed her way. Time to go below. She grabbed Max's hand, tugged him with her.

"What are you doing?" he asked when she finally let go.

"Someone is watching us." She checked the portholes but none of them gave her a decent sight line. "They had binoculars. I think the ship was *Ladyslipper.*"

"No worries. That's Reggie Perkin's boat." Max shook his head, his smile irrepressible. "I told him I couldn't make the annual voyage up here this fall. He's probably wondering why I'm here now."

Relief rushed over her, burned her cheeks as Callie realized she'd just given him a firsthand look at the nerves she'd always kept hidden. "Oh."

"I haven't seen any sign of *Windchaser* and I did keep an eye out for her when we were coming in. I think maybe we've lost her—at least for now."

"Maybe."

They went topside, spoke to Reggie and hired a mechanic to repair the prop. All the time Callie kept up her surveillance but she couldn't shake the feeling that someone besides Reggie was taking an interest in their every move.

Max rented a car and drove to the outskirts of town.

"This is about as far as you can go. There are no roads out of Juneau. It's completely waterlocked. But you can't come here and miss the Mendenhall Glacier," he told her. "It's too beautiful."

In the parking lot, several buses were picking up their passengers while more kept arriving.

"It looks like a popular place." A thick blanket of blue-white ice glinted in the morning sun. Little rivulets ran off it into a huge lake. The wind carried a frosty bite from the glacier.

"It is popular. If you're interested we could go white-water rafting. The river is frigid but the guides make sure you don't get dunked."

"I think I'll pass and save my energy for something more—restful." That creepy feeling raised the hair at the back of her neck an inch higher, but though she scanned each face they passed, she could see no one she knew.

"Okay, then. There's a pretty good path around the lake that leads to the glacier, we'll try that. Just stay away from the edge."

"No problem. I like swimming but not with icebergs." She grimaced at the bits of ice floating in the water. They didn't appear to be melting at all.

"So what's the next step to finding Josiah?"

"Don't know yet. Wait, that's my phone." She stepped to the edge of the path to read the text message. "This afternoon I'm to take the tram up Mount Roberts. An operative spoke to Josiah yesterday, told him I was coming and why. Josiah has a friend that operates the tram. He said he'd leave word with this guy where we could meet."

"I'm going with you."

"No, Max. You're not. This is the end of the trail." Fury backlit his seafoam eyes so she hurried into speech. "It's not that I'm ungrateful for all your help. I am, truly. But this could get dangerous. I don't want you caught in the middle." *I don't want the guilt for hurting someone else.*

"I can take care of myself. Haven't I proven that to you yet?"

They were drawing too much attention. Callie slipped the phone back into her pocket, linked her arm in his, drawing him toward the glacier.

"Let's just go look at the glacier."

He walked beside her but she could feel the tension in him.

"Why do you keep doing this, Callie? I could help you, I *have* helped. Yet you keep pushing me away. I want to know why. What are you so afraid of?"

In this at least she could be honest.

"I'm afraid that you'll get hurt on my watch. This isn't your job, Max. It's mine. I'm used to taking what comes. I know how to handle myself. I know what my reactions will be. But I can't gauge yours. I can't prepare you for something when I don't know myself what's going to happen. That puts us both in danger." She drew in a deep breath. "I don't want you to get in the way."

"In the way? Is that what I am to you?" he asked, his voice barely audible. "In the way? Well let's fix that right now."

In a second he'd pulled away from her. His lips pursed together in an angry scowl.

"I'm going to the information center. It's over there. Meet me when you're ready. I don't want to get in your way."

He turned and left, taking long, giant strides away from her. He'd misunderstood—but Callie didn't call him back. It hurt to watch him leave, but it was better this way. Risking his life in a situation over which she had no control—it wasn't going to happen.

She turned back to the path, walked toward the glacier. Some people were climbing onto the ice but she wouldn't be one of them. The thick mass of blue-brown ice had ruts and chasms where streams had melted it. Too easy to slip, get caught in one of the openings.

A nearby guide explained features of the glacier.

"The ice ranges over two hundred feet high and recedes at a rate of ninety feet per year. With global warming we're expecting the ice to melt much faster in the next ten years."

Her phone cut off the next part. Callie stepped to one side to let someone pass as she answered.

"Callie, we're checking out this man Max said he saw watching you in Ketchikan. I was hoping to talk to Max personally, maybe get some more details, but his phone isn't working or something because I can't reach him. Is he there with you?"

"No. What have you learned, Daniel?"

"Actually next to nothing. Peter asked around Ketchikan but couldn't find anyone who recognized the guy. We've done comparisons using computer reference points of the face against mug shots on file but nothing's come up. Not surprising, I suppose. The pictures just aren't that clear."

"And he's wearing a cap," she agreed. "That means shadows."

"Yes. Can you think of anyone who might be after you?"

She could, but he was in jail.

"No."

"Rats! I was hoping you might come up with a name."

"Sorry. I'll just have to pay more attention."

"Yes, you will. Be very careful. We've dug into Aaron Eade's financials with a fine-tooth comb. Our forensic accountant says he's carrying a lot of debt and there's word on the street in L.A. that he's into a couple of loan sharks. Men like that get desperate, do nasty things to get money."

"I'll be careful." She hung up. A different tour group was scattered along the path, discussing the lake, its brilliant blue-green color and frigid temperature. She had to step around some of them to get past where the path narrowed because of big boulders. "Excuse me," she repeated over and over.

One group of men didn't budge. Since she couldn't go behind them, she had to find purchase on the sharp rocks along the path. She'd almost made it when a hand touched her shoulder.

"Payback," a voice whispered. Then the hand shoved hard and Callie found herself falling face-first into the lake.

Callie thought she screamed but the breath left her body as soon as the icy-cold water bit into her skin. It seeped through her clothing as if she wore gauze. A warning voice in her head reminded her she only had a few moments before hypothermia would set in. Then she would die.

She struggled to reach the rock in front of her, forcing her weighted legs to move, but the rock was wet and slippery and she couldn't get a grip.

"Grab this." Max leaned out over the water, threw her the end of his jacket. "Hang on, Callie. Just hang on."

Her teeth were chattering so badly she couldn't speak. When the material floated near she forced her hand open, stuck her fingers into the loop he'd made. They seemed to freeze around the coat. She couldn't have let go if she'd wanted to.

"Hang on, Cal. I've got you." Slowly but surely he dragged her to shore, then pulled her up over the rocks.

"C-cold," she stammered, wondering why the sun didn't feel warmer. Her arms and legs dragged like logs. They wouldn't obey her orders.

"Somebody help me get her up. We have to get to the car. The heater will help."

Max took her left hand, a stranger grabbed her right. Someone else placed their palms under her shoulders. They shoved her erect. Callie had to hang on or fall over because her legs didn't work. Neither did her arms. If only her teeth would stop chattering, she'd tell them that.

"He pushed her in. I saw it."

"Who?" Max glanced around. But nobody knew where the perpetrator had gone. "It doesn't matter. Let's get her into the warmth."

Somehow they got her to the car. Max turned on the engine, hit the fan button so it poured air into the vehicle. After he'd thanked the others he climbed in beside her, began undoing her jacket.

"You have to get this off, Callie. We'll deal with the rest at the boat but for now get this off. It's sopping wet. The heat can't penetrate it."

That was two coats she'd ruined. She let him pull it off, too cold and weak to do anything but shudder. The heat blasted her face but it didn't penetrate to her body.

"Just hang on. I'll get us to the boat. You'll be in the shower in no time."

Her head ached and something was dribbling onto her face. Pressing her lips together to stifle any noise, she dragged one hand up to touch her forehead, found it wet and sticky. She must have bumped against one of those sharp rocks. At least her hands worked.

By the time they got to the marina, Callie had regained some of her strength. Not enough to walk without help, but enough to insist she'd undress without his help. Max ignored her protests, shoved her into the shower with all her clothes on. She wanted to argue but the water steaming off her body felt so heavenly she swallowed everything but a squeaky "thank you."

When she finally emerged from the shower draped in a towel, Max wasn't there. But some of the clothes he'd ordered for her in Ketchikan lay on the bed. She dragged them on, dried her hair. Her movements were slow, her limbs leaden. At least she was no longer freezing.

She found Max in the galley putting together a pot of steaming hot chocolate. She accepted a mug from him, cuddled it in her hands and sank down on the sofa, curling her legs beneath her. Max draped a quilt over her.

"Hurry up and swallow that so we can go to the doctor."

"I don't need one, Max. I'm fine." Only then did she notice how white his face was. "I'm fine, truly."

"You have a cut on your forehead."

"I think I must have grazed a rock when I fell in."

"You didn't fall. Someone pushed you."

She nodded. Truth time.

"I need to borrow your phone. Mine's at the bottom of the lake."

He handed it over, then leaned one hip against the counter and watched her dial.

"It's Callie, Daniel. I've lost my phone. You'll have to contact me through Max's for now. I need you to run a check on someone. Terhan Stone. I thought he was in jail but someone just pushed me into a lake and I'm pretty sure it was him."

"He's the guy Max saw?" Daniel asked.

"I don't know. I haven't seen him in years."

"How do you know him? I don't recall the name from your file."

"It's a long story." Please let him be satisfied with that.

"Okay, we'll run him and let you know. Can you make it to Mount Roberts for two o'clock? Maybe I should send someone else?"

"I'll be there."

"Just be careful. I'm glad Max is there. He can watch your back."

"Yeah." She glanced at her husband, noted that his usually tanned skin had not yet regained its color. "Max pulled me out. I'd have frozen to death if not for him."

Daniel gasped. "This is getting way too dangerous. Maybe we'd better call it off."

"Not on your life," she told him grimly. "If Terhan Stone is involved in this, there's no telling what he might do to Josiah. He has a habit that needs money constantly. Or he did."

"I'll check him out. Talk to you later."

She'd have preferred the conversation to be private but that couldn't be helped. She'd just have to hope Max would listen to reason. There was no way she would let Terhan get anywhere near him. No way at all.

"Are you feeling warmer?" He'd switched on the heat. The room was gloriously, beautifully warm.

"I'm feeling toasty." She set down the mug. "I never said thank you for pulling me out of there."

"Did you think I wouldn't?" A lopsided grin enhanced his good looks. "I wasn't that mad."

"I thought you'd gone to the building," she whispered recalling the horrible sinking sensation as the numbing cold took over.

"I was about ten feet away. I looked around. When I glanced back you were in the water. They said you were pushed, Cal."

"They were right. He put his hand on my shoulder and said 'Payback,' right before he shoved me forward."

"Then you didn't see his face?"

She shook her head, watched his eyes narrow.

"Then how do you know—?"

"Let's just say I never forget a voice." She so did not want to go into this now. Ever.

"You've never talked about this man, the name is too distinctive. I'd have remembered." His face tightened. "Not that you ever talked about your work much. Always the secrets."

"Let it go, Max." She said the words softly, praying he'd stop asking questions she couldn't, wouldn't answer. "I have to be up on Mount Roberts to see Josiah's friend by two. We could stop and get something to eat along the way unless it takes a while to get there."

"You don't want to tell me how you know him."

"No." She set the cup down, folded the quilt and rose. "I just want to get on with this job."

He sighed, but after a moment nodded. "Fine. You

catch the tram at the cruise ship dock. But let's have lunch first. There's a terrific little café I know with the best homemade soup. You'd better put on another sweater."

Callie picked up a gorgeous blue sweater that fell to her hips, picked up her backpack, then stepped up to view the area around them. A prickle of awareness told her that somewhere Terhan waited and watched. She couldn't suppress a shiver.

"Are you still cold? I could rent a car, drive a few blocks. But we'll see more if we walk."

"I'd rather walk." It's easier to get away. "Tell me about Juneau."

"What do you want to know?" He matched his step to hers.

"Anything."

"It has a history of gold. In 1880, two prospectors, one of them named Joe Juneau, made Alaska's first gold strike in the rainforest along the banks of the channel called the Gastineau. They named it Gold Creek and the camp grew by leaps and bounds." He checked to see if she was listening. "Until the last mine was shut down in 1944, this was the world's largest producer of low-grade ore."

"Here it's flat but it feels like we're pushed up against the hills behind."

"That's because all the flat land stretching from downtown where we are, to the airport, is landfill from mine tailings. The only way out of here is by air or water." He stared down at her, his eyes darkening. "If this Terhan was on *Windchaser*, that's how he got here."

She nodded, mentally assembling pieces, tossing those that didn't fit.

"I can't help but wonder how Aaron Eade figures into this. As far as I knew there was never a connection between him and Terhan."

"Except that you said you hadn't seen him for years."

"True."

"Anything could have happened."

Max's phone rang. He glanced at it, handed it to her. "It's Daniel."

"This is Callie."

"I'm going to e-mail you a picture of Terhan. See if Max recognizes him, will you?"

"Okay. What else did you find out?"

"He was given early release two months ago. He's been living in Vancouver, checking in with his parole officer every week, as ordered. Until this week. Nobody's heard from him lately."

"Is there a connection between him and Aaron Eade?"

"Not that we've found. But get this. Apparently Aaron has been communicating with Josiah for at least six months. Some of his coworkers remember him talking about taking a trip to see his former stepfather—soon. Everyone in the office thought the two were on good terms. Apparently Josiah even flew in for a visit last week."

"What?" Callie frowned. "I thought Josiah Harpnell was some kind of recluse."

"He likes his privacy, he works in the wilds. But there was nothing to stop him from going to see Eade if he wanted to."

"It doesn't sound right. Why go now when he's supposed to sign some papers?"

"Don't ask me. Maybe the fellow you talk to this afternoon will be able to shed some light on things."

"I'll find out what I can," she promised.

Max's hand on her arm stopped her from walking any farther.

"This is the place," he said.

Decorated in a rustic mountain theme, the café boasted the aromas of food prepared on-site. Roast chicken and stuffing, a full-bodied pasta sauce and cinnamon-scented apples were three Callie identified.

They were shown to a booth against a window. Both ordered the special. Once Callie had her tea and Max his coffee a strange silence fell between them.

"So?" Max quirked one eyebrow up in a question.

"I don't think—"

"You're not going to shut me out now?" he asked, his eyes turning a richer shade of green. "Not after we've come this far?"

"It's not a matter of shutting you out, Max. Believe me, I'm very grateful for everything you've done. But it can't continue. This is my job. I've already broken about every rule in the book by having you accompany me. It's dangerous and I don't want you hurt because of me. I need to do the rest on my own."

He shook his head, leaned back against the seat, rested his hands in front of him on the table.

"I'm beginning to think there's something you don't want me to know."

"Really?" She swallowed the fear, dragged on nonchalance. "There are a lot of things you shouldn't know. This is still a confidential matter."

"On which Daniel allowed me to accompany you. I think I can be told what you've learned about this Terhan fellow."

Callie debated the wisdom of letting him get too close. Once she met the tram guy, she was determined to do the rest on her own. Max would go back to Victoria. And for him everything would go back to normal.

"Well?"

She told him what Daniel had relayed, paused when Max began shaking his head.

"No way," he said firmly.

"What?"

"It couldn't have been Josiah in L.A."

"Why?" She waited until the waitress had served their meals. "How do you know that?"

"Josiah doesn't fly. Not ever. I read that in an article about him."

"Whether or not Josiah flew, I still don't see how Terhan and Aaron could be working together. What's the connection?"

"I guess we'll have a chance to ask questions after we take a tram ride."

A few minutes later the waitress handed Callie a long brown envelope. "A man asked me to give you this."

"Me?" Callie glanced around. "Who?"

"He's gone."

"You're sure it was me?" She watched the other woman nod. "Okay. Thanks." She slid her fingernail under the flap.

"From Finders Inc.?"

"There's usually the logo on their stationery." She opened the envelope, glanced inside and froze. Every single nerve in her body turned to ice, a numbing sensation much stronger than that she'd experienced in the lake. She struggled to free herself.

"Callie? What's wrong?"

"Nothing." She closed the envelope, licked the flap hoping it would stick shut. As soon as she could, she'd burn it.

"It's not nothing. You're white as a sheet. Let me see." Mac reached out to take the envelope from her fingers.

"No!" Callie reared back, shoved it into her backpack. "It's—top secret," she hissed. "Not for your eyes."

"But it's to do with this case, right? Can't you tell me?"

She shook her head. "Sorry. I can't."

Max ate in silence, but every so often he stared at her in a hard, penetrating way that told her he hadn't bought her explanation.

"We might as well go to the tram," she said when they were outside. "There could be a line and I'd like a chance to poke around beforehand."

The walk to the tramway was silent.

"What is this man's name?"

"Sam McKee. Isn't that funny?"

"Huh?" Max didn't get it.

"*The Cremation of Sam McGee* by Robert Service. Famous poem taken in high-school Lit. Don't tell me you don't know it?"

"Oh. Yeah, I do."

No point in belaboring it. Callie bought their tickets. There was no lineup so they climbed into cars adorned in colorful Tlingit artwork. As they glided up 1800 feet through the Alaskan rainforest, Max pointed out the Chilkat Mountains to the north, the Gastineau Channel, Douglas Island on the west and Silver Bow Basin in the east where gold was discovered in 1880. Callie caught her breath at the beauty before her.

"Untouched creation," Max murmured against her ear. "God at His best."

She twisted around to stare at him. He always brought God into it.

"I've been praying He'll help you figure this out without anybody else getting hurt."

Yes, that's what she wanted, too. But if the contents of that envelope were any indication, Terhan wasn't going to let bygones be bygones.

She had to get Max out of here. Fast.

His phone rang again.

"I forgot. Daniel's e-mailing a picture of Terhan for you to identify."

He studied the phone's small screen for several minutes.

"I think it's him."

"Good." She text-messaged back the confirmation.

The gondola jerked to a stop. Callie stepped out. Unsure of exactly where she was to find Sam, she followed Max to the Mountain House, nestled among towering Sitka spruce trees on the edge of grasses and wildflowers of the sub-alpine.

Though she longed to relax and enjoy the culture and beauty with him, she couldn't shake a feeling of urgency. At Raven Eagle Gifts she asked a young native girl about Sam.

"He just came off lunch. That's him, over by the tramway."

They walked over to a short bristled man who was scolding a teen for littering.

"Are you Sam McKee?"

"Have been for sixty-two years."

"I was told you could connect me with Josiah

Harpnell. I have some documents for him to sign. Is he staying at your place?"

Sam wore a funny look. "What's your name, lady?"

"Callie Merton. This is my husband Max. Is something wrong?"

The man frowned, looked at Max then beckoned them both to follow him to an open spot outside where no one could overhear.

Callie's radar immediately went up. "What's wrong?"

"That's what I'd like to know. Can't you make up your mind or what? Josiah's not a young man. He shouldn't be trucking all over the place at your beck and call."

Callie glanced at Max who shrugged.

"Sir, I don't know what you're talking about. Please explain."

"Josiah got a telegram yesterday. From you."

"Not from—"

Max shook his head at her, turned to Sam. "What did this telegram say?"

"That she couldn't make it here and he was to get himself to Skagway fast. That it was a matter of life and death."

Terhan? Or Aaron?

"I didn't send any telegram, Sam." She met his scrutiny without flinching. "We've been sailing from Ketchikan to Juneau especially to meet him. When we were delayed by the fog, I was told you'd be here at two to direct me to him."

"Look, lady. The message had your name on it. I should know. I got it right here." He shuffled through his pockets for several moments, finally pulled out a piece of paper. "They hand delivered it to me here. I told Josiah right away. Had to take some time off to do it."

"It's very important we catch up to him." Callie scanned the paper. The telegram was as he'd described, including her name at the bottom. "When did he leave?"

"Yesterday morning."

Her heart sank. They were a whole day behind.

"How did he leave?" Max asked giving her a sideways glance. "Did he fly there?"

Sam shook his head vehemently. "Josiah doesn't fly. Not ever. Some guy offered him a ride on his boat. Older fellow we know, earns his living taking guys from the Lower 48 out salmon fishing. I forget his name."

At least it didn't sound like Aaron, or Terhan.

"Thanks a lot." Callie turned to leave, then changed her mind. "Just one more thing. Do you happen to know if Josiah went to see his stepson a couple of weeks ago? In California?"

Sam hooted with laughter. "Josiah Harpnell—in California? No way."

"Maybe he didn't tell you about it, maybe he was embarrassed," Max suggested. "Weren't they estranged or something?"

"Don't know about that. Never heard Josiah talk about the kid. But he wasn't anywhere near California, that I can guarantee. Hates the place. He was over in Denali."

"Denali?"

"It's a national park," Max murmured in her ear.

"He's been updating his research into migration patterns now that talk's heating up about that pipeline again. He's been there for the past three months. Summer's his best time. He sure wouldn't waste it trotting off to that place. Anyway, he hates the heat."

"Okay. Well, Sam, thank you for telling us."

"No problem. When you find him, remind him I'm having Christmas this year. No way I'm going through that pass to get to his place when it's thirty below. His cooking's not *that* good." He cackled a laugh, then went back to work.

Though Max was speaking to her, Callie heard little of what he said. She was too busy trying to come up with a way to get to Skagway. According to the radio report she'd overheard in the tramway building, the airport was filled with people who'd missed their flights for two days. It wasn't likely there'd be any open seats to Skagway.

That left Max and the boat.

"Callie?"

She glanced up from the moss she'd been staring at. Max's eyes had darkened. Something was wrong.

"Finders just text-messaged for you to call in. Apparently Josiah phoned them to ask for help. Someone attacked him last night."

"Can you take me to Skagway?"

"Of course. No problem."

But it was a problem, especially with Terhan in the picture.

And it was going to get worse.

NINE

With Callie safely aboard and on the phone, Max went back to pay the man he'd hired to keep watch on their boat.

"You got the prop fixed?"

"Of course. You sure messed it up."

Max didn't want to do any explaining. "Anybody snooping around? Asking questions?"

"Nary a one." The offer of cash payment was quickly accepted and pocketed.

"Thanks a lot, Fred."

"You let me know if you need me again, Max. Haven't seen you up here in a while. Everything okay?" Fred's attention was on Callie.

"Sort of. We're trying to find someone. Josiah Harpnell. Do you know him?"

"Sure. Got some parts for Josiah this spring. Took 'em up on the White Pass Railroad. He's a good guy. Sure cares about what happens to the north."

"Yeah." Max thought a moment. "Why the White Pass?"

"Easiest way to get to his place is to ride up out of the valley on the railroad. You get out at the top, then go overland from the international customs building. Two miles east is a trapper's shed. Josiah usually spends the night there if it's cold or stormy."

"Is his place nearby?"

"No." Fred scratched his head. "It's a pretty good trek from there to his cabin on the Yukon side. I don't do it often. Neither of us is getting any younger but Josiah travels a lot faster than I do. 'Course he's used to it."

"Okay. Well, thanks for the help."

"No problem. Oh, I almost forgot. Mary White-feather delivered this. Said you'd asked for it." He handed over a bag.

Max glanced inside, nodded. "My wife got pushed in the lake at Mendenhall this morning. Lost her coat. I thought one of Mary's jackets would keep her warm."

"Bad place to swim. Hope your lady's feeling okay."

"Thanks." Max waved then returned to the boat. Callie sat on a bench seat, watching him. "This is for you." He tossed her the bag.

"It's beautiful." She fingered the thick wool. "It looks handmade."

"It is. By a friend of mine. She sells her things in the stores locally. I thought you might like a memento of Juneau. Ready to cast off?"

She nodded so he quickly freed them of the dock, and using the motor, which now purred contentedly, he directed their craft away from Juneau.

Callie spent a while on the phone, then she returned it to him. Whatever she'd learned hadn't cheered her up. She looked dispirited as she glanced over the water with little interest.

"Do you need me for anything up here, Max?"

"No. Why?" He checked her face, noticed the pasty whiteness of her cheeks. "Are you sick?"

"No. Just very tired. And my shoulder hurts. I thought I'd go lie down for a while."

"Go ahead. Nothing about this fellow Terhan yet?"

"Nothing more than I already knew. Apparently he came up for parole and some bleeding heart listened to his sob story. He got out way too early."

"Sorry." He checked his controls. "We should pull into Skagway sometime this evening if we don't run into any trouble."

She gave him an odd look. "Don't even think it."

"Figure of speech. Stop worrying, Cal. We've got God on our side. Go and rest."

She nodded without saying anything, descended below decks. After a few minutes, Max heard no sounds of movement.

His phone lay on the dash. He debated the wisdom of doing what he intended, then finally grabbed it and dialed.

"Daniel? I want to know what you sent Callie in that envelope."

"Good to hear from you, too, buddy. I'm fine, thanks for asking."

"Sorry." Max bit back the retort he had ready. "I know you're up to your ears there but I'm working in the dark here and it's frustrating. Callie got your envelope while we were having lunch and she turned pea-green. Wouldn't let me see it, just stuck it into her backpack. So I'm asking—what did you send that could have such an effect?"

"*I* didn't send her anything, but let me check." Silence reigned for a few moments then Daniel came back on the line. "Neither Shelby nor the front office sent anything. There's no record of anything from Finders going to her. Are you sure it was from us?"

Callie had mentioned a mark. Max remembered that Finders Inc. put a watermark on all their envelopes. Max could not recall seeing that mark on the envelope the waitress had given Callie.

"If not you, Daniel, then who?"

"I think you'd better talk to Callie about that. And whatever you do, don't tell her you called me. She'd be furious."

"I know." Max hung up, concentrated on getting them to the entrance to Lynn Canal. At least Callie was getting some rest. Hopefully he'd have gotten past his frustration of being kept in the dark by the time she wakened.

Nothing about the trip was going the way he'd hoped. Instead of opening up, she'd become more secretive than ever.

And Max was starting to wonder if he'd ever know the truth.

Callie made sure the door lock was tight, then lifted the envelope from her backpack. She didn't bother to check inside, she knew it was there.

It had to be from him. He was baiting her, sending this to scare her. And it did, but not for the reasons that he thought.

She had to get rid of it.

Callie glanced around the room. Smoke detectors dotted the lower-level ceilings. A fire on board was everyone's nightmare. The smoke alarms would certainly bring Max running. So she couldn't burn it. What else? Overboard? No, that was risky. Somebody might find it—somebody like Max.

The oven.

She unlatched her door, slipped out and into the galley. A roaster was tucked under the small oven. She lifted it out carefully, trying not to make a sound. Once it was in the oven, she lifted the lid, set the envelope inside and replaced the lid. She eased the oven door closed and set the temperature at 500 degrees.

But after a few moments an acrid smell began to fill the small area and she had to shut off the oven or risk answering questions. What now?

She glanced at the fridge. The bare bones of an idea began to bubble.

Callie pulled open the door. Someone had restocked. A package marked Arctic Char lay on one shelf beside lemons. If she grilled the fish for dinner, she could use the barbeque up top. You had to warm up a barbecue before using it. The envelope placed inside would ignite and burn off long before she put the fish in.

Callie straightened the kitchen, returned to her room and hid the envelope. Then she lay on her bunk. But her conscience would not be silent.

Max deserved to know the truth. She claimed she wanted him out of her life, but she was still here with him. She'd asked him to leave but all she really needed to do was to show him that envelope.

Once he saw what it held, nothing and no one would keep him anywhere near her.

"Callie?"

She was crying.

Max touched her cheek, hoping to wake her gently

from the bad dream. But she didn't really waken. She leaned her wet cheek into his palm while the tears rolled down her cheeks.

"He was so small," she wept. "So tiny and so precious."

She was dreaming about the baby. An arrow of pure pain pierced his heart. Whatever Callie had said about having a family, she'd wanted their baby. He knew that more surely now than he ever had.

Max sat down on the side of the bed, slid an arm around her, drew her against his chest. She laid her cheek against the soft knit and sobbed for all they'd lost.

"Don't cry, Cal. It'll be all right."

She'd fully wakened. Now she blinked up at him, teardrops dangling like crystals from the end of her lashes.

"How is it going to be all right, Max?"

"I don't know, but I know that God heals if we let Him."

"Don't talk to me about God," she sniffed.

"I have to. Because I think that's the only way you're going to come through this. Both of us."

He eased a hand over her curls, brushing them back to press his lips against her forehead. It felt so right to hold her in his arms again, to finally share the pain of losing the most precious thing they'd ever had.

"We have to accept that we don't know the reasons why, but that He works things out for the best. He wasn't punishing you or me or the baby. He was doing what was right. Because God is love."

"You sound so sure," she whispered.

"That's about the only thing I am sure of," he admitted. "God will take us through the pain if we keep trusting Him to work it out. That's His promise to us."

"I didn't want him to die, Max. There are a lot of

things I'm not sure about but that isn't one of them." Her eyes pleaded with him not to judge.

"I already knew that, Cal." He gazed into her face, amazed at the rush of love that filled him.

What would he do without her? He couldn't think about that. Not now.

"You would have been a fantastic mother. You *will* be."

"Thanks." She shifted away, suddenly shy. "The day before I left, you were gone to that boat show, remember?"

As if he could forget.

"I had an ultrasound that day. They gave me a picture." She peeked up at him through her lashes. "Do you want to see it?"

His heart burgeoned up into his throat. Max nodded.

"It's in my backpack." She scrambled around him, off the bed and snatched up the tattered blue sack. She dug through the main pockets, finally pulled out an envelope. "Here it is."

Was this what the waitress had given her? No wonder she'd gone white. But no, she'd had the picture for a while judging by its worn edges.

"I tried not to crease it. Look." She sank down beside him, held out the black-and-white sonogram.

Max couldn't move. He stared hard at the image, gulped. *Please God, oh please help me not to question You now.*

"Can't you see him?" Callie's head bent, one delicate fingertip traced the tiny head. "Look here—eyes, nose, mouth. He's sucking on his fist. The other arm's here."

No mother had ever displayed more pride. It hurt to watch her outline the tiny limbs with such tenderness.

Her hushed voice, almost bemused, pointed out every feature lovingly.

"I see, Callie."

"I named him David." She tilted her head to look at him, drenched eyes huge in her waiflike face. "Is that okay?"

"It's perfect."

"He was perfect." The tears came again but this time Max thought they were healing tears, assuaging the hurt that would be a long time dissipating.

"Yes, he was perfect." He took the picture, set it aside and cupped her face in his hands. "But we have to let him go now, Callie. David's not ours anymore. He's God's. He wouldn't want you to be sad. David would want his mother to smile whenever she thinks of him playing on green grass, sleeping on a cloud, resting in the most capable arms there are."

"But—" She bit her lip, glanced at the night stand. "How do I do that?"

"By trusting. By believing that even the worst thing in the world can be used by God to bring something wonderful into our lives. Let's honor David, not mourn him."

"I can't just forget what happened, how he died," she burst out, her sapphire gaze cloudy with suppressed emotions.

"Of course not. But to keep going over and over his death, the horror of it—that dishonors him. Let's think of him with love because he's in a place full of it. Nobody could love our child more than God Almighty. Not even us."

She watched him for a long time, studying his face, searching for something Max couldn't explain. Finally she sighed, nodded.

"I'll try."

"Good." He scrambled for something to break the tension. "We're in Skagway, but we don't have any more leader yet. Let's have dinner. I've already grilled some fish. We can eat on deck. It's certainly warm enough tonight."

"You cooked?"

Something—fear? flared in her eyes.

"Yes. You were resting so I thought how nice it would be if you woke up to a hot meal. You've prepared them for me often enough. You'd rather go out?" he asked belatedly, wishing he'd thought of that earlier. Maybe Callie didn't want to be near him.

"No. No, it's fine. Great, in fact." She dredged up a smile that didn't quite reach her eyes. "It's just that I had planned the same thing. Great minds, I guess. I'll go clean up."

She turned, squeezed past him, and left the room. A few moments later Max heard her footsteps overhead. He glanced at the sonogram, took one last look then slipped it into a drawer. They had to move on. Surely she'd see that now?

But as he slowly mounted the stairs he couldn't help but wonder if she'd ever really open up to him. Would there ever come a time when she looked at him without that cloud of fear?

Please God?

The next morning Callie found another envelope while Max was shaving. This one was taped to the helm. A scrawl of words across the top made her skin crawl.

Time to pay up.

Pay up how?

She tore it up into bits, put them in a can and burned them, praying Max wouldn't finish shaving before the last bit of evidence was gone. When only black ashes remained, she relaxed, made coffee and carried it to the prow where she sat sipping as she scanned the area.

But though she prodded her brain relentlessly, Callie found nothing that would tell her what Terhan planned next. Her phone rang.

"Callie?" Daniel's voice sounded weary, as if he'd been up all night.

"Yes?"

"Josiah left a message. He's gone back to his place."

"What?" Callie listened to the rest, closed the phone and started planning.

"Good morning, gorgeous."

Who could resist a grin like that? Callie smiled, motioned to the cup and thermos she had left sitting on the table.

"Good morning. Coffee's ready," she told him.

He poured himself a cup, sat down across from her. "What's on the agenda for today?"

"Actually I just finished talking to Finders Inc. about that. Josiah's fine. He wants to meet us at Yakutania Point. But I'm going to need your help."

"Mine?" Max's dark eyebrows rose in disbelief, but after a moment he shrugged, nodded. "Sure. Whatever I can do."

"After we eat, I'd like you to go to the point yourself. Wait there for Josiah."

"And you'll be doing what?"

"I want to scout the area alone, make sure no one is nearby. Once I'm sure neither of you were followed and that Terhan isn't around, I'll join you both. We'll bring Josiah back here to sign the papers, then figure out the next part."

"Okay." He studied her face. "Do you think he'll go back to his cabin? Will he be safe there?"

"I'm hoping to talk him into coming back with us until police can catch his stepson and Terhan and question them both."

Funny how the lies rolled off her tongue so easily. Had she become too used to playing someone else, too comfortable burying her own identity underneath another persona that she couldn't even feel bad about lying to her own husband?

No, the guilt was there, buried. But she was doing this for Max's benefit. Better to remember that.

"When do you want to start out?"

"In half an hour you should leave. It's not a long walk according to Shelby. You should have lots of time to stroll around. Keep an eye out for Aaron and Terhan."

"And you?" A ripple of concern feathered his forehead with small lines. "How will you get there?"

"I'll slip into the shops, put some kind of disguise together. If I'm not there by noon, you bring Josiah back here and take him to Finders. Okay?"

"Noon? But that's—"

"Can you do it or not, Max?"

"Yes," he said after a long pause. "I can do it."

"Thank you." Relief washed through her like a river.

"Don't thank me yet," he warned. "We'd better get some breakfast."

"I never eat before going out. My stomach is too busy doing backflips to digest anything. I should probably be over that by now but I'm not."

"Some cereal," he suggested. "That should settle it."

She shook her head but he ignored it.

"It's going to be a long day no matter what happens, Callie. You'll need to keep your energy high. Please, just try."

"Fine." She stayed topside while Max went below. She needed the time to sort through the details. She couldn't afford to make a mistake.

"Here. Try this." Max handed her a cereal bowl with a mixture of granola and fruit swimming in milk.

"Thanks." She'd never be able to eat it all, but she swallowed a few spoonfuls, then carried the rest downstairs to dispose of before he could comment. She checked her backpack, made sure everything she'd need was there. One glance at her watch told her it was time for Max to go. She moved upstairs, pasted on a confident smile.

"I'm ready," he told her, his green-blue eyes swirling with things unsaid. "Are you sure this is going to work?"

"I'm positive. Just watch your back. If you think something doesn't look right, call the cops." She held up his phone. "I'm going to keep this for now, if you don't mind. Finders is supposed to call me back in twenty minutes."

"I don't need it." He laid his hands on her shoulders, his gaze locked with hers. "Please be careful, Callie. There's a lot of money at stake and I don't think those two men care much about hurting people. They're dangerous."

As she well knew.

"I'm always careful, Max. Always."

"Will you promise me something, Cal?"

"If I can."

"When this is over, when we're back in Victoria, before you accept another mission—will you meet me, spend some time talking things through?"

"Max, there's nothing—"

"There's everything to talk about. I won't push you. I won't bully you. But we need to make some decisions—together. Promise?"

"All right," she said, conscious that the minutes were ticking away. "If at all possible, I promise I won't leave town before talking to you. Satisfied?"

"Not nearly." He bent, brushed his lips against hers in a sweet, soft caress that started a throbbing ache in her heart. His hands cupped her face, his eyes full of—love?

"Promise me one more thing."

"Max—"

"It's important. If you get in trouble, if you need help, if you can't think what to do—I want you to remember that God is there. Doesn't matter if you can't feel Him, just know He is. And He'll help. All you have to do is ask. Okay?"

She nodded, not because she thought she'd be calling on God soon, but because she wanted him gone. This was too hard.

"See you later, sweetheart. I love you." He kissed her once more, then was gone, striding toward the town in that sure, confident gait that was pure Max.

Callie felt something on her cheeks. Tears. She dashed them away, furious at her own silliness. Agents for Finders, Inc. didn't cry!

She gathered her things, tucked the phone into her pocket and locked down the boat. Ten minutes after

Max had left she followed. Her first stop was a general store to get the supplies she'd need. Second stop—The White Pass and Yukon Route Railway. She had five minutes before the train would leave the station.

Callie checked for the hundredth time but no one had followed her. Which meant one thing.

They'd already left town, ahead of her but behind Josiah—an old man traveling unprotected through the wilderness.

"Please let him get home safely," she whispered. "Please. And take care of Max."

If it took begging to get God's help, she'd beg for the man she now knew would never leave her heart.

"Passport, please."

Callie handed it over. The customs official gave it a cursory glance, then studied her backpack.

"You're hiking in?" he asked with a frown.

"To see a friend."

"Then you should know we've got weather reports suggesting this nice weather isn't supposed to last. Do you have some means of contact if you run into trouble?"

She nodded. "I'm all set."

"We don't get many women hiking alone up here." He checked his computer, then asked for her weapon. "I see you work for Finders Inc. I hope they've prepared you adequately?" It sounded like a question. "Are you up here on a mission?"

"I'm hoping to locate a Mr. Josiah Harpnell. We need his signature on some documents."

"Good luck." He stamped her passport and handed it and the gun with the permit back to her.

After replacing her gun, Callie stepped outside the international customs building, checked her compass and headed toward the small hut she could see in the distance. She'd received instructions to Josiah's place from a park ranger but this territory was boggy and too easy to get lost in. Fortunately some kind of a trail made it easier to follow.

Walking up here was like strolling the edge of Heaven. Through the tips of the trees she saw valleys, rivers, waterfalls. Beauty beyond anything Callie had ever imagined. It reminded her of Max's words about their baby playing in Heaven.

She passed the trapper's shed about two hours before dark. Thoughts of staying there were quickly dismissed when she smelled signs of a recent skunk's visit. Callie pressed on.

With the sun's descent she was forced to take cover in a small clearing next to a stream or risk traversing the rough terrain and perhaps missing the path. Then, too, there was a danger of falling or otherwise getting injured.

Thick, ferny spruce provided a fragrant cover over her lodging spot. Callie built a fire, ate some of the dried food she'd packed and sipped water from the plastic bottle she carried, mentally noting each one of the night sounds of the forest around her.

She wondered what Max would say if he saw her here, like this. He'd always claimed camping wasn't his forte, but he'd always gone—just for her.

She missed him, missed hearing his soft reassurances, the gentle brush of his fingers against her skin, the feeling of knowing he was there and he cared.

What was he doing now? He'd have read her note,

realized she'd deliberately left him behind. No doubt he was hurt—and furious.

Callie thrust the image of those pained eyes away, dredged up her usual habit of pretending to be someone else. Who would it be tonight? A woman on her way to the Klondike Gold Rush? Part of a troupe preparing to entertain men who'd been panning gold for months? It always seemed easier to pretend to be a part of the past than of the present.

But when the moon slipped out from behind a cloud and illuminated the forest floor she was forced to admit her old method of avoidance wasn't working. She didn't want to be someone else tonight. She wanted to be Max's wife, sailing the Inside Passage, sharing his life.

Going undercover was just her job. It wasn't who she was.

Callie sat up straighter as the truth filtered in. Pretending to be a woman who eagerly sacrificed everything for the sake of her work was a mirage that did nothing to fill the hole in her heart. Somehow she'd turned her missions into fairy tales—tried to fool herself into believing she didn't want a husband, a family, a life apart from work.

She did. She wanted them so badly. But she didn't deserve them.

Maybe once she got Josiah to safety, turned Terhan in to the authorities—

A huffing sound thirty feet away dumped Callie back into reality. She froze, listened.

A bear.

Soon they'd be in their dens for the winter, but this year the berries weren't particularly good and the bears, still hungry and missing the cold weather, were late hibernating, according to the ranger she'd spoken to on the train.

Callie had heard reports of them ransacking camps, stealing food, attacking campers. Best to be prepared. She slid her fingers to her belt, pulled out the knife she'd fasted there. She'd use her gun if she had to but it would be preferable not to alert anyone in the area to her presence. Bears prefer their own company, she reminded herself.

The puffing sounds of the animal grew louder. Callie pressed her back against the tree and pushed herself erect. Less than a minute later a brown bear ambled into the clearing. He sniffed, stopped, looked at her.

"Get out of here," she hollered as loudly as she could, clanking her knife blade against the tree and squeezing her empty plastic water bottle so it crackled with noise. "Go!"

The bear stared at her for several moments then obligingly turned and padded away, snorting as he went. She waited until the forest returned to its previous silence, her heart rate slowing bit by bit.

Max would have loved seeing that.

Sternly she ordered herself to forget Max and get back to business. If she could make Josiah's by noon, she could get his signature and head out again right away. Unless he was hurt.

Memories of Terhan's past violence tumbled through her brain. Callie pushed them away. She had no hard evidence that Terhan was involved in any of this. Nothing but that niggling suspicion that would not go away.

She sat for a long time, watching the fire, adding more wood as needed, and occasionally lapsing into thoughts of Max. Her shoulder itched where the stitches had dissolved. She rubbed it against the tree, glad she'd chosen the two entwined trunks as her backrest. With the fire in front and her supplies strung overhead, she was relatively safe here. She looped her backpack over her good shoulder to use as a pillow.

The snapping twigs burned quickly thanks to a frisson of wind that chased across the clearing. She added two more sticks and then a bigger piece of rotted wood she'd saved especially for the night hours. It should hold till morning.

The hours dragged past. Callie's eyelids drooped, blinked open, then sagged again. She decided to sleep, just for a few moments.

The crack of a tree branch awoke her. But that was all she heard.

Suddenly the world went black.

TEN

Her head ached like the very dickens.

Callie pried open one eyelid at a time, winced at the brilliant sunshine filtering in through the one small window.

Where was she?

"Finally awake. I didn't think I hit you that hard."

Facts began sinking in. Her hands were tied. She scanned the room, found the source of the sardonic voice.

"Aaron Eade, I presume."

"You are good." A lazy half smile tipped up the corners of his lips. "I'd like to say it's a pleasure to meet you, but, well, it isn't."

"Same here," she muttered, fingered the sore spot on her head. She stopped when she saw him pawing through her backpack. "Hey!"

"Ah. I knew you'd have it safely tucked away." He slid out the papers Josiah was to sign. "I'll take the liberty of handling this for you," he said with a laugh. "You being indisposed and all, I don't suppose you'll be able to make it very far. Besides, I have this newly prepared will that also needs signing."

"Naming you as beneficiary, of course."

"Who else?" He shrugged. "After that it's simply a matter of tying up loose ends."

"You're going to kill Josiah." She shivered at the evil in his eyes.

"Not at all. I'm no murderer. I'll just sit and wait. He's old. He won't be here forever."

"You can't afford to wait too long," she reminded him. "Your, er, creditors, are getting anxious."

"You've been doing your homework." A nasty smile turned his handsome face ugly. "You should have minded your own business."

A noise outside sent him whirling toward the door. He pulled it open, glanced out, told someone to wait, then closed it again. Aaron strode over to her, dragged her upright.

"I do hope you'll excuse my bad manners, but I have some private business to conduct and it does not involve you."

Callie had no time to struggle as he pushed her into a tiny room at the back of the cabin.

"Make a sound and you'll be sorry," he said right before he shut the door.

Callie leaned her head against the door and listened. He had company and it sounded like they were arguing. A door slammed. They must have gone outside because she couldn't hear anymore. When she tried her door, it wouldn't budge.

Callie sat on the floor, tried to think what to do. She had to get to Josiah before he did. She couldn't have another death on her conscience.

"Sorry—"

The door flew open. Callie tumbled backward, sat

down with a hard thump, wincing when her shoulder hit the wall. Aaron's smile turned ugly.

"Trying to listen in, were you? Naughty girl. Go sit over there."

Since he had a syringe in his hand, Callie obeyed, praying desperately that he wouldn't drug her. Of all things she'd endured on her missions, this was the one thing she'd feared most.

But Aaron didn't appear interested in sticking her. He waited until she sat, then wrapped a rubber hose around his arm.

Callie glanced around the room, searching for the papers Finders Inc. wanted Josiah to sign. They were gone.

"Aaron! Where are the papers you took from me?" she asked. If only she could get an answer before the drug—whatever it was—rendered him totally out of it.

"Don't worry." The needle dangled from his vein, his eyes grew glossy, his movements slow, languorous. "That's all going to be taken care of."

"How?" she asked. His speech had started to slur. She watched his eyes, realized the drugs had already hit his bloodstream. "How will it be taken care of, Aaron?" This time she raised her voice.

He blinked at her, smiled.

"I've got it all worked out. No problem."

A sudden rapid pounding leeched away his smile. He pulled out the needle and let it drop while he brought up his arm to stem any bleeding. With an awkward jerk he lurched to his feet and started toward the door. Callie sucked in her breath as he narrowly missed hitting a table. He stumbled several times before he finally grasped the doorknob and dragged open the door.

There was no one there.

Aaron didn't look outside, in fact he wasn't looking anywhere. He clutched at his throat, his eyes widening when no sound would come out. His breathing changed to a guttural gasp.

"What's wrong?" she demanded but he couldn't tell her. "Help!" she yelled at the top of her lungs. "Help!"

Max loomed in the doorway, a big stick clutched in one hand. "Callie? Are you all right?"

She'd never seen a more welcome sight.

"Yes. Quick, untie me, Max."

Once he ascertained Aaron was no threat, Max dropped the stick, used his pocketknife to cut her free.

"What's wrong with him?"

"He just injected himself. I think he's having a reaction." She knelt alongside Aaron's prone body, checked his pulse. "It's too fast," she muttered, then reached down to slap the man's cheek. Maybe he wasn't too far gone yet. "What was in the needle, Aaron? Coke? Crack?"

His head thrashed from side to side. "Hero—" He passed out.

"Heroin?" She kept her finger at the side of his neck, counting out the beats. "It's slowing," she told Max.

In fact Aaron's breathing was now quite shallow. Too shallow. He must have injected too much. Or the drugs were contaminated. She didn't have enough information to guess which.

"Will he be okay?"

"I don't know." Callie straightened, peered into that beloved face. "What are you doing here, Max?"

"You need to ask?" He glared at her. "I'm here to help, despite your little disappearing act."

"It's too dangerous. I wanted you out of it, Max." She couldn't stop staring at him, savoring every line and angle of his handsome face.

"Too late. I'm here. Just in time, I'd say." He shook his head at Aaron's prone body. "Don't bother telling me to go away because there's no possible chance of that happening. Not now."

Callie opened her mouth, then paused. Why pretend?

"I'm glad you came," she murmured.

"You are?" He blinked, reached out to trace the rope marks on her wrist.

"Yes, I really am. Thank you." Time to concentrate on business now. "Someone was here earlier, Max."

"Who?"

"I couldn't tell who it was. Aaron locked me in a closet. But while they were here they took the papers I was to have Josiah sign. I think they also gave Aaron that needle." She bent, checked his pulse again. "It's too faint but I don't know what to do. I can't call anyone because your cell phone doesn't work in this valley. But to leave him here—" She shuddered.

"Wait a minute." Max's eyes darkened. "Heroine." He grasped her arm, pulled her upright. His stare met hers, steady, unflinching. "You think the mystery guest was Terhan."

She nodded.

"I don't know why or how, but yes, I think this all ties into him. Terhan always had drugs for sale when I knew him. Maybe he was supplying Aaron. Otherwise, what's the connection between them?"

He nodded, his face thoughtful.

"It makes sense. The only question is: was that

needle deliberately tampered with?" He searched her eyes. "So what now?"

"Now I have to get to Josiah."

A movement caught her attention. Something was going on with Aaron. She pulled her arm from Max's grasp and hunkered down, trying to remember every bit of first aid she'd ever learned.

"His breathing isn't right."

Max squatted beside her, pulled up an eyelid. "Look at his pupils. He's overdosed, Cal. There's nothing we can do for him now."

A few gasps of air and Aaron was gone.

Callie balled her fists at her sides as Max got a blanket and laid it over the body. Another life ruined thanks to Terhan. When would it end?

"What do you want to do now?"

"I'm leaving." She grabbed her coat from where Aaron had hung it.

A quick check of her pack showed most of her supplies were gone. Perhaps he'd left them at her campsite, used them or simply tossed them. Either way all there was left was her water bottle, a few granola bars and two instant coffee packets. The brown envelope the waitress had handed her still lay secreted in her bag—where it would stay until she could burn it.

She sifted through Aaron's gear and found little that would help. A packet of matches, a tattered sleeping bag that she'd have to take because hers was gone and a small photo of a woman taken years earlier. His mother? She left that with the rest of his things.

"Do you want something to eat? I brought some supplies." Max pulled out an orange, handed it to her. "You'd better eat something before we set out."

"We?" She peeled the orange keeping her gaze on him.

"I'm not going back, Callie. I don't know who or what Terhan is to you, but he's dangerous. You may need help to get Josiah out. I'm that help."

Tears filled her eyes. After all she'd done—the tricks she'd played—Max was here, still willing to help her. She was crazy to let him go.

"Thanks," she whispered.

"No problem." He smiled and her heart took off as if it was airborne.

Callie tried to tamp down the joy but she couldn't. She'd dreaded the next part, still did. There was no telling what they'd find. But with Max there—

Fool! Her brain kicked in. Max might look at her with love now, but he wouldn't once Terhan knew who he was. Max would hate her after that.

But she couldn't, wouldn't give up when there was a chance that another man might die.

"It's looking very dark outside. I think a storm might be blowing in." Max helped her put on her pack, followed her out of the cabin to a spot under a tree. He'd tied his own pack high up in the branches. "According to the forest ranger I spoke with last night, Josiah's place is about ten miles due east of here. It's quite rough terrain."

"I'll be fine, if that's what you're hinting." Actually her head ached like fury. She was glad the clouds had rolled in because the sunlight only added to her discomfort.

"Well, not only that. The ranger seemed to think a snowstorm was imminent." He met her skeptical stare and shrugged. "Hey, he lives here. He should know the signs."

"But it's only mid-September."

"Callie, up here they can have snow in July. This is the north country."

"Yeah." She set off following the path of broken twigs and crushed grasses that someone had used not long before them.

"At least he left us a trail," Max murmured.

"That's what bothers me." Callie chewed her bottom lip. "He could have covered his tracks a lot better than this. So obviously he wants us to follow." *Because he wants you to pay for what you did.*

It wouldn't be long before she'd come face-to-face with Terhan, tonight, maybe tomorrow. Then the pretending would be over. Terhan would make sure all her secrets were exposed. That's what those envelopes had been about.

He was warning her that this time she couldn't pretend or hide. There would be no going undercover this time.

Callie forced herself to keep going even though her head ached abominably. Max called a halt at noon, beside a small mountain stream that bubbled over black rocks. Mountain sheep stood in the middle of it, downstream about two hundred yards. They seemed only mildly curious about their visitors, more interested in quenching their thirst.

"Here." Max held out a sandwich. "I made them before I left. Smoked turkey."

"Thank you." It was her favorite sandwich and he knew it. She took a bite. It tasted like ambrosia, her water like nectar.

"Didn't you pack any food?" he asked.

Callie tried to read the expression in his eyes but he

sat in the shadow of a huge spruce tree and she could discern nothing.

"I did. Aaron must have eaten it. I didn't find much in his stuff." She put the sandwich in her lap as her mind filled with the memory of his prone body. "I wish—"

"Don't go there, Callie. There was nothing you could have done."

"I know." She knew it was from the stress, the bump on her head, but she couldn't help shedding a tear for the man. He hadn't deserved to die.

"Come on. Finish your sandwich. We've still got quite a ways to go." Max took a long drink, glanced at the sky. "What are you going to do once we get there?"

"Well, it's not like we can launch much of an attack. I don't think Josiah has a whole bunch of neighbors who'll help, either." She'd been muddling over the same problem for the last two miles. "There's not a lot to do but walk up to the door and knock. You could stay back and assess the situation. Nobody will be expecting you."

"I'm not so sure you're right." He had hold of her arm and refused to let go.

Callie glanced at him, then down to see what had snagged his attention. A steel trap lay on the ground, its metal jaws jagged and ready for the first negligent limb.

"A trapper's line—here?" A quick survey of the area around them revealed no more of the deadly things, but that didn't mean they weren't there.

"It's not part of a trapper's line, I don't think." Max hunched down for a closer look. "This one hasn't been used in a while. These traps have been banned for years. See the rust here?"

"I see it." Callie shuddered. "Blood poisoning at the ready."

"Yep. And no hospital nearby, either." He snapped the lethal teeth together using a stick then carried the contraption to the base of a big tree where he placed it upside down. "That was deliberately set, Cal. Which means he knows you're coming."

"Of course. I told you, didn't I? He visited Aaron when I was there."

Terhan's face as it had been that long ago day in court swam into her mind. The words were as clear now as they'd been ten years ago.

"He's hoping I won't get as far as Josiah's. He's hoping I'll die out here."

"One of these days you're going to have to tell me why this man is out to get you." Max tipped his head back and swallowed water from his bottle, but his eyes never left her face.

Callie pretended nonchalance but inside she was a mess of trepidation.

"I'll tell you when you explain how you know about traps," she muttered before turning back to the trail.

"That's easy. A friend of mine from college lived in Alaska. I came up for a New Year's visit. He explained it to me then."

"Oh."

He loped along beside her, obviously waiting for her explanation.

Well, he wouldn't have long to wait. Terhan would take great pleasure in explaining her past in vivid detail—unless she could keep Max away from him.

They walked until the sun had almost disappeared

over the eastern ridge, until they spotted Josiah's cabin in the distance. Callie was dead tired and her headache still hadn't gone away, but she wouldn't stop until she was sure their campsite was well hidden from the cabin's view.

"I think we'll stop here for the night," she murmured.

"You don't want to keep going?"

She shook her head. "It's got to be another four miles and I'm too tired to walk it and have any reserves left to fight him. Besides, I don't know what else he's laid out to trap us. I'd rather wait till daylight."

"Okay." Max slid off his pack, sat on a big boulder looking as fresh as if he'd just left his condo.

Callie ignored him, tramped the area to gain familiarity. When she was satisfied that they were below the ridge and virtually invisible thanks to their thicket of towering spruce, she finally slid off her backpack. Max was already gathering fragrant cedar boughs for a backrest and to sit on.

"It's getting colder," he said. "That snow may yet be on the way. Especially at this elevation." He squinted at her, tilted her face to the light. "Are you all right?"

"Headache. I'll be fine."

He pushed her hair back off her face, feathered his fingers over her scalp. Callie couldn't suppress the wince of pain when he encountered the bump on the back of her head.

"He hit you?"

"Last night. I was camped, had just chased away a bear. I fell asleep. When I came to, I was in that hut where you found us."

His mouth tightened to a thin angry line, merely let his hands drop away.

"I brought an ax. I'll get some firewood. I have a hunch we're going to need it tonight."

"No fire. He'll see our smoke."

Max shook his head. Pointed upward. The sky was already darkening, partly because of the thick clouds that were crowding in. Across the valley a mist crawled up the mountain sides in a thick concealing shawl of deception.

"He won't see anything through that fog. He might smell wood smoke but that could be coming from anybody in the area."

"Like?"

Max was busy laying tinder for a fire, but he paused for a moment, smiled at her.

"It only feels like we're alone up here, Cal," he murmured.

Since they hadn't seen anyone else during their trek here, Callie assumed he was once again talking about God. She turned away, concentrated on unpacking her few essentials. Max did the same.

He was much better prepared than she was. Not only did he have an axe but he'd managed to include a solar blanket, a small radio and a couple of tins of food, which he was opening with his knife.

"We'll let the fire burn down a bit then I'll heat up this soup. I don't know about you but I'm hungry."

Since her stomach was gnawing at her spine, she could only lick her lips in response and watch the glowing embers flicker and dance in the breeze.

They ate the soup slowly, taking turns sharing the

can. Max rinsed it out, then poured in some water and set it among the coals.

"I have a couple of tea bags, and you have instant coffee," he reminded.

"That'll warm us up." She leaned back against the tree trunk and struggled to find the right words. "About tomorrow—you need to be prepared for anything, Max."

He studied her. "Tell me what you can."

"Understand that I haven't seen or heard from Terhan Stone in a very long time. But he was in prison and I expect that changed him." She drew in a breath of courage. "He also has a hate on for me because I testified against him. Judging by what's happened so far, Aaron's death among other things, I'm guessing he doesn't care who he hurts as long as he gets what he wants."

"And what he wants is for Josiah to sign those papers making him—what? An heir?"

"As far as I can tell that's it." She shrugged. "I don't understand why or how he got his knowledge about this. How could he know to get to Aaron or hope to carry the whole thing off? The thing I'm worried about most, though, is keeping Josiah safe. That has to be my main concern."

He nodded, his face thoughtful in the firelight's glow.

"You said 'among other things.' What other things, Cal?"

Here it came.

"He's left things for me. That envelope the waitress gave me, at the boat—he's been baiting me. I think it was he who sent Josiah that telegram with my name on it."

"That sounds really serious—to carry revenge that far?" He shook his head, obviously puzzled. "Whatever you sent him up for, it must have been huge to keep him mad for so long."

"Yeah." She needed to divert his attention. "Anyway, that's why I'm asking you to stay in the background. Watch and listen. If something happens you can hike out for help or until you get a signal on the phone." She leaned forward. "I can't let Josiah be hurt, Max. I expect that Terhan has probably knocked him around a little, maybe even drugged him. But I don't think he'll kill him unless he's already got what he wants. From what I've read about Josiah, I don't think he'll give in easily."

"Won't Terhan realize he'll be a suspect—especially if he's a beneficiary?"

She smiled but felt no mirth.

"That's why he won't want to leave witnesses. He'll cover his bases quite carefully. And after all, what proof do I have?" She poked the fire with a stick, watched the flames flare, then die down again. "I'm sure the story will go something like this: Someone must have attacked Aaron, killed him, then moved on to Josiah."

Max remained silent for a long time. Callie didn't disturb him, knowing he needed time to absorb what she'd said. Max's world had nothing in common with hers. He designed boats for the rich and well-heeled of the world. Thugs like Terhan and his way of getting what he wanted were as foreign to him as mobs and guerilla warfare.

That's why she knew he'd be horrified when Terhan finally told him her dirty little secret.

"I think we need to pray about this, Cal."

In the old days they'd done that a lot. But things had changed.

"I don't have a lot of faith in God anymore, Max."
She risked a sideways look at him. "Not since the baby,"
she whispered.

His head was bent, his focus remained on the fire.

"I know what you mean."

He didn't. He had no idea of the depths of her despair.

"You can't—"

"My mother was diagnosed with a very aggressive
cancer this past year."

The words took her breath away. So did the pain she
now glimpsed in his eyes as he stared at her.

"I stood there watching as the treatments wasted her
body away—and I could do nothing. I was utterly
helpless to do a thing to help my own mother." He
gulped. "There is nothing more humbling on this earth
than to watch someone you love suffer so horribly."

"Max, I didn't know. I—I would have come if—"
She stammered to a stop at the fierce glint that turned
his eyes to hardened steel.

"I'm glad you didn't. I'm glad you weren't there
to watch it." He jammed his fist against his leg, his
face twisted as he stared into the flames. "You
couldn't have done anything, Cal. Nobody could.
Except God."

Something in the way he said that grabbed her by the
throat. She needed to hear more.

"God let it happen. He sat in His Heaven and He let
my mother suffer terrible pain. And all I could do was
watch. And try to pray. But how could God do that?
How could I truly believe He had her best interests at
heart—and let that happen?"

She'd thought he couldn't understand her pain. How

stupid she'd been. Max had gone through his own private agony and she hadn't even known about it.

"Dad and I took turns sitting with her. Most of the time she was too drugged or too sick to know we were there but we couldn't just leave her alone." He sighed, leaned back, stretched out his heels. "I sent Dad home to rest but I'd spend countless nights sitting by her bedside, scouring her Bible for some ray of hope that would help me understand why. I begged, cried, pleaded—all to no avail. I couldn't find a reason for her suffering. Not one that satisfied."

Max was quiet for so long Callie feared his next words.

"What happened, Max?"

He looked up as if startled, met her gaze and smiled. "My mother happened. She gave me a lecture I'll never forget."

Fiona Chambers was a passionate woman. She'd always taken life seriously, as if she had to squeeze every drop out of the days she was allotted. But Callie could think of nothing even Fiona could say that would help Max.

"She was as sick as a dog. Her bones protruded from her wrists. Her hair was gone, her makeup, too. She'd developed an allergy. She couldn't stand without help and walking was impossible." Max shook his head.

Callie caught her breath at the glow of love shining in his eyes.

"She looked like a skeleton, but she demanded to know what was wrong with me. Once I'd told her she grabbed me by the chin and said, 'Look, kid. Either God is who He says He is and He knows exactly what He's doing here, or the Bible and everything else you've believed in for all these years is a lie. You'd better decide which and make up your mind to stick with that decision no matter what happens.'"

Decide which. The words found resonance in Callie's heart.

"They took her for another treatment then and she couldn't talk till around two the next morning, and then it was only a croak. But the words she spoke are as clear in my mind now as they were then." He closed his eyes, recited so quietly she had to lean forward to hear.

"'Faith isn't something you can put down and pick up again when you need it. Faith in God means believing in His love despite all the evidence to the contrary. The one thing I hang on to now is the fact that God loves me. Nothing else much matters.'"

"She was very strong," Callie whispered.

But Max shook his head.

"She wasn't, God is." He touched her cheek, his eyes alight with his discovery. "That's when I made my decision, Cal. That's when I decided that God is exactly who He said He is, that He does what He says He does and that I have to trust that somehow He'll make it come together."

"But—"

He shook his head.

"There aren't any buts. It's a take it or leave it deal. Take it, believe it, accept it and go on. Or leave it and spend the rest of your life asking the same questions, getting the same answers." He rummaged in his pack for a moment, pulled out a tiny testament. "Listen. 'The steps of a man are established by the Lord; and God delights in his way. When he falls he shall not be hurled headlong because the Lord is the One who holds his hand.'" He turned a page. "But this is my most favorite verse. 'He is their strength in time of trouble.'"

The serenity she saw in his eyes wasn't something he'd faked.

"You see, it doesn't say there won't be any trouble. It says God will be our strength. We can depend on Him. You can depend on Him."

Could she? Terhan, the past, the secrets, the pain— all of it towered over her like a pile of bricks just waiting to tumble and crush her.

"I used to believe. But I don't know if I can get that back again," she whispered, loving the warm touch of his hand against her skin.

"Don't go back, sweetheart. Go ahead. Trust God today. And when tomorrow comes, you trust all over again." He wrapped an arm around her, drew her against his side. "God loves you. He has for a very long time, not because you're good or smart or any other reason. He simply loves you, and He offers that love knowing everything there is to know about you."

She frowned. Everything?

"He knows those secrets you won't share with me. He knows what happened on the missions you kept so silent about. He knows how much you wanted the baby. He even knows you're mad at him. But none of it matters to God. He loves you anyway."

Callie felt the press of his lips against her hair.

"You're thinking about reasons He can't love you, aren't you?"

"How did you—" She tipped back to search his face.

"Because I'm beginning to understand the way you

think." His eyes met hers and refused to look away. "You can't believe that there is love that won't disappear just because you do something wrong. I love you, Callie. More than anything in life, but even I don't love you as much as God does. There's just one thing you have to know."

He traced her eyebrows, ran the tip of one finger across her cheek, touched the corner of her mouth.

"What?" She felt breathless caught in the steady glow of his eyes.

"Nobody can make you accept that love. Either you reach out and grab it with both hands, accept it. Or you decide it isn't for you, that you're the exception, and you let it go. It's your choice."

He snuggled her close again, his chin resting on her head.

Callie knew he was praying. But she couldn't.

Max didn't understand. What had happened, what she'd done—it wasn't something you wiped out with one wave of your hand.

He'd know that soon enough. Terhan would make sure of it.

ELEVEN

"Okay, here we go. Unless I stand in the doorway and wave, you will not come into Josiah's cabin. Agreed?"

Max nodded. It wasn't what he wanted but Callie was the expert here. He had to follow her lead or risk—who knew what?

"Good." But she remained where she was, watching him.

"What else?"

"Nothing. Just—thank you for doing this."

He didn't want her thanks but Max accepted it with a shrug, touched her lips with his fingertip.

She bent over, checking the small revolver at her ankle.

"Callie?"

"Yes?"

"Be careful."

"I will." She gave him one last look.

Max couldn't decide what he saw in her eyes. He puzzled over it while watching her dart from one tree to the next.

They'd circled in by the back way to get a better look around. There wasn't much to see. Josiah had some kind of a shed, which was firmly padlocked. There were two big mounds near it but those were covered with tarps and he couldn't identify what lay underneath. Probably the man's research equipment.

Callie lifted her hand, pointed at the door. She was going in. He held his breath as she crept across the wooden veranda and laid one hand on the doorknob.

Oh, Lord, be with her now.

A moment later she'd disappeared inside. He waited, checking his watch frequently. Five minutes. Ten. Fifteen. And still no sound from inside.

An eerie stillness descended on the land. Maybe that feeling came from the lowering clouds that promised precipitation, or maybe he was just on edge. Either way Max scanned the area constantly, looking for something, some sign that would tell him what to do.

Crunch!

A twig snapping echoed sharply in the cold air. He sucked in a breath and pressed himself against the trunk of the tree. Moments later a man stepped into the clearing in front of the cabin. He carried a shotgun and walked with sure, firm strides toward Max.

Fifty feet away he stopped, aimed the barrel of his gun directly at Max's hiding place and fired.

Max had time for one thought before the pain knocked him down.

"Be with Callie, God. Please be with Callie."

The shot reverberated around the valley like a repeater rifle.

A bullet of fear pieced her heart but Callie refused to give in to it, wiped the sweat slicked forehead of the man on the narrow bed.

Josiah moaned.

"Hush now," she whispered. "We've got company."

What was Terhan firing at? A wild animal—or Max?

She hurried out of the bedroom, scanned the tiny interior and tried to decide her next move. Terhan had obviously drugged Josiah. The cabin was low in provisions. Maybe he'd gone out to shoot some game and was now coming back.

She dragged the heaviest thing she could see—a handmade pine table in front of the door, blocking its entrance. The small window was another matter. Josiah didn't have anything that high. But there were three long boards he used as shelves. She shoved whatever was on them onto the floor, stood the boards up so they covered the window, then pushed the old worn horsehair sofa in front to hold them up.

"Not great but better than nothing," she muttered. "What else?"

The fire. Josiah had a big black wood stove. It still radiated heat but inside most of the wood had burned down to white coals. The barely open damper added to her impression that Terhan hadn't been here for a while. He'd wanted the fire to burn slowly.

Callie remembered a stack of wood piled just outside the door. Only a few pieces were inside. She could burn them if she had to. But if Terhan got onto the roof, he could cover the chimney and smoke them out.

Callie opened the damper fully then tossed the dishpan of water she'd been using to wipe Josiah's forehead onto the coals and quickly slammed the door shut. She waited for several minutes then checked. Most of the smoke had dissipated. Good.

Now all she could do was wait.

* * *

Ignoring the pain ripping through his shoulder, Max grabbed the lowest limb and hoisted himself into one of the spruce trees shielding him. His jacket was a deep navy and the hood he'd pulled over his head helped him blend into the shadows. His green pants melded easily among the trees. He wouldn't be easy to spot on this dull day.

Max moved upward slowly, going as high as he dared while keeping Terhan in his sights at all times.

The killer hadn't moved. He stood staring into the trees as if searching for his quarry. If he bothered to look closely Max knew he'd find signs of blood on the pine needles, but either Terhan hadn't known what he was shooting at or he didn't care.

He held his breath as Terhan stepped forward, obviously intending to investigate. But a loud thud from inside Josiah's cabin averted his attention. He frowned, walked to the door and pushed on the handle.

The door didn't budge.

"Trying to lock me out, Callie?" The sneering tone carried clearly to Max. "You know it's not going to do any good. I want the old guy's signature and I'm going to get it. One way or the other."

Terhan might have supplied Aaron with drugs but Max was fairly certain he himself wasn't high, not now anyway. He sounded cold, determined and intent on reaching his goal. It took every ounce of resistance Max could muster not to lower himself to the ground and make a run at the guy as he baited Callie. But he had to choose his time. Callie was all right as long as she remained inside, away from him.

"Open this door!" Furious now, Terhan kicked at the

thick planks with his heavy army boots—to no effect. The door did not give an inch. He stepped back, changed his tone. "Come on, baby. Open it now. You know I always get what I want, Callie. Always."

The taunts irritated Max with their unspoken insinuations. Terhan sounded as if he and Callie had a connection that went beyond fugitive and witness. He wondered how the two had come to know each other.

"You wanna be like that—fine. Let's see how the great secret agent handles herself now." Terhan cast one last indignant glare at the door then walked over to the shed. He blasted off the lock, disappeared inside.

The seconds ticked off. When the other man didn't immediately reappear, Max decided to climb down, relocate. He'd barely laid his foot on a branch when Terhan burst out of the shed, a red metal can in his hand.

He was going to burn the cabin—with Callie and Josiah inside!

Please God, no.

Max held his breath, watching in morbid fascination as the other man began to dribble gas across the veranda.

Suddenly he knew what to do. While Terhan talked trash to Callie, Max eased himself down the tree, moved deeper into the woods and worked his way around to the back. From previous reconnoitering with Callie he knew there was a window there. Maybe he could get inside— do something.

The acrid odor of burning gas and wood filled the air. Terhan seemed so involved with dousing the door of the building he never even bothered to check the yard. Which was good.

Max made a dash for the window, tried to grasp the bottom with his fingertips. It was too high.

"Callie!"

She had something over the window. He grabbed some stones, tossed them at it. Eons later her beautiful face appeared. She must be standing on something. She slid open the window.

"He's got the front on fire. You'll have to climb out. I'll break your fall."

"What about Josiah? I can't just leave him." She thought for a moment. "Maybe—"

"Isn't this sweet? A reunion." Terhan leaned against the corner of the cabin, his shotgun pointed directly at Max's chest. "Open the door, Callie. There's a fire extinguisher in there. Use it on the front porch. If you don't I'll blow a hole through him."

She never answered. Terhan moved the gun two inches to the left and fired, grazing the side of the building not six inches from Max's arm.

"Now, if you don't mind. Unless you want to see hubby die."

A scrabbling sound came from inside, then the sound of something heavy being dragged.

"That's my girl." Terhan's grin was pure evil. He stepped forward, prodded Max. "Move, buddy."

Max walked around the building, saw Callie spraying out the last of the flames. She'd pushed the rain barrel over just to make sure nothing else burned. Puddles of water dripped off the steps onto the ground.

"Inside, both of you."

Max glanced at Callie, tried to apologize with his eyes. He should have rescued her. Now they were both in danger.

"Sit down." Terhan waved the barrel at the sofa, waited till they were seated. "Long time no see, baby. Too long."

Callie stared at the other man as if she found it hard to recognize him.

"Why are you doing this, Terhan? Josiah never did anything to you. He's just an old man trying to make the world a better place."

Max longed to tell her to save her breath. Men like Terhan didn't listen to reason. But maybe she was just trying to talk him down, looking for an opportunity to pull her own gun.

"I'm not doing anything. Haven't you heard? He's my stepfather." Terhan laughed at her blink of surprise. "A crack agent like you and you didn't figure it out? It's all about the estate, honey."

"But you're no relation to Josiah."

"Sure I am." He chuckled, relishing his own little joke. "Stepdaddy and I are as close as two peas." He reached into his pocket, pulled out a pair of glasses and put them on. One hand scraped his hair back off his face, smoothed it down. When he spoke again, his voice had softened. "You're not the only one who can do undercover, sweetheart."

The resemblance was uncanny. A change of clothes, a little makeup and Terhan could easily pass for Aaron.

"It was you," Callie whispered, her eyes huge with disbelief. "You went to L.A. as Josiah. You met with Aaron, maybe even took his place."

"Of course." Terhan's cruel lips lifted in an ugly grin. "We had to iron out some details and I needed to practice. I'm good, Callie. But then I've had a long time to plan."

"How long have you been planning this?" she asked softly.

"Long enough to make sure every detail is taken care of. I've thought of everything, Callie." He watched her, his eyes intent on sharing some unspoken taunt. "I had lots of time to do it, thanks to you. But I didn't waste a minute. I've kept track of you ever since I went into the joint. I even have pictures from your wedding. Such a handsome couple. It pays to have friends on the outside."

Max felt as if slime had just hit him. The guy was carrying out a real vendetta. And they had no backup.

"You had something to do with the other firms failing to get Josiah's signature, didn't you, Terhan?" Callie was focused on the moment. "You wanted Finders to be hired. But how could you make sure I'd get the job?"

"Timing," he told her, his face harsh in the kerosene light of the cabin. "Every detail perfectly planned for the ultimate result. Except for Iraq. I hadn't planned on you going to visit Daddy. You hadn't been in touch with him for years. What sent you rushing over then?"

Visiting her father? In Iraq? Max twisted to stare at her.

She squinted. "Your nose is different. You had plastic surgery."

He barked out an angry laugh.

"You try living in that hole where you sent me, you'd need plastic surgery, too."

"But that's not why you had it."

"Of course not." His eyes flashed daggers. "Don't change the subject—which, by the way, was Iraq. What were you doing there?"

She pretended blatant unconcern. Max was almost fooled—until he glanced at her fingers, saw how white the tips had gone where she gripped her jeans.

"Finders Inc. sent me. It's my job."

"You never did courier work before."

Callie shrugged carelessly. Max was certain Terhan couldn't see the tic in her neck.

"I go where they send me. They sent me there."

He appeared appeased for the moment. Then he slid a long brown envelope from his jacket. Callie's envelope?

"It's time to get business done. I want his signature on these papers and I want it now. I'm not playing at this, Calliope. I intend to inherit that estate."

"You won't get away with it." She paled at his laugh. "What are you going to do to Josiah?"

"Kill him, of course. Then you two."

They needed a diversion. Max twisted, looking for something to deflect the murderer's attention and buy Callie more time.

"It's snowing," he told them, peering out the open door.

An vicious grin licked up the corners of Terhan's lips.

"Perfect. By the time anyone finds any of you, you'll be skeletons. Or bear bait." He held out the envelope. "Go get the signature, Callie. Then sign that you witnessed it. Nobody will question Finders Inc.'s best agent. Your signature will seal the deal."

He watched her rise, walk toward him. He tapped the rifle barrel against her shoulder.

"But before you go in there, I want your gun."

"I haven't got it." She stepped back, avoiding the slap he would have laid against her cheek. "Max had it. He must have lost it when he fell out there."

Max stared. He'd never had it. Then he realized she was playing Terhan.

"Do you think we wouldn't have used it by now if we had a gun?" Max demanded, seething that this creep dared assault Callie. "I'd use it on you in a heartbeat."

"Ah, yes. The loving husband defending his lovely wife. I wonder how much you really know about your darling Callie, Maxwell."

He was insinuating something. Max glanced at Callie. Whatever it was, it had her scared. She stood as if frozen to the floor.

"There's nothing you can tell me about Callie that I don't already know."

"Really?" Terhan looked surprised. He stared at Callie. "You told him about our little tête-à-têtes? And he doesn't mind? How modern of him."

Max struggled to suppress the wave of confusion those words brought. What had Callie said—that she'd helped put this man in jail. Suddenly he wished he'd asked more about how she'd helped accomplish that.

Terhan watched them like a bird watching his prey.

"Perhaps she didn't quite tell you everything, hmm?"

"Don't Terhan. Please."

She was begging him. Max glanced from one to the other. Something was going on, something that raised every warning bell in his system. Another secret. He kept his face impassive, reluctant to let the creep see that he'd hit a nerve. If he just waited long enough, surely the truth would come out.

"Your pretty little wife had an interesting youth, Maxwell." Terhan's smug little smile testified to his pleasure in baiting Callie. "Very interesting. She's not quite the lily-white you thought, you know."

"I know everything I need to know about *my* wife." A cold fury engulfed Max. Why hadn't she told him, prepared him? Her secrets had placed him in this position.

"Oh, I doubt you've heard all of the story. For instance—did you know she used to work for me?"

His breath gagged in his throat but Max refused to blink and give the guy any satisfaction.

"You don't believe me? But it's true. Here, I'll prove it." Terhan dragged Callie's backpack closer, pulled something out and tossed it at Max. A picture. "That's your sweet little wife posing for me. I must tell you, a lot of men liked that picture."

Max couldn't bring himself to look at it. Instead he squeezed his fist together, crushing the ugliness.

"I'll get the signature." Callie's voice had lost all animation.

"I thought that might motivate you." Terhan moved to the doorway, varying his gaze from Callie to Max. "What's the matter, hubby? You don't look so happy."

Several suggestions hovered on the tip of Max's tongue. He swallowed them all, concentrated on taking an inventory of the room, praying that it would help deflect the increasing burn from the wound in his shoulder.

Terhan had already said he was going to kill them. Gunshots left evidence. One bullet could be explained as a hunting accident. Any more would arouse suspicions. Which meant he had something else in mind.

Why didn't Callie use her weapon?

"He signed it." Callie stepped out from the bedroom, handed the papers to Terhan. "What now?"

Terhan spent several moments checking the signatures.

"What's that mark beside your name?"

"My confirmation as a notary that Josiah's signature is true and freely given." She pressed her lips together.

"That stung, didn't it?" Terhan was exultant. "Honest Callie told a lie. Or should I say another one." He grinned at Max, folded the papers and shoved them into his pocket. "Well, folks, it's been real. But I have to leave you now."

He backed toward the door.

"I'm sorry it had to come to this, Maxwell. But getting involved with Callie—well, that was just bad news all around. Still, you should try to make peace with each other before you die. Take a look at these. At least you'll have something to talk about in your last hours."

He flung an envelope across the room. Callie snatched it up, thrust it quickly into her backpack, which he'd tossed on the floor. Her actions confirmed everything Max feared. But he said nothing, kept his eyes on their captor and watched helplessly as Terhan stepped through the door, slammed it shut. A loud thud reverberated around the cabin.

Max raced toward the door, tried to pull it open. It wouldn't budge.

"Why didn't you shoot him?"

"Because I had no clear shot that would have stopped him from firing that rifle at least once." She glared at him.

A few moments later smoke began to seep under the threshold.

"He's going to burn it," Callie muttered. "We have to get out of here."

"Fine by me. Any idea how?"

Her blanched face wore a determined look. "I have no idea. But I'm not just going to sit here and die."

A noise from the other room drew their attention. Callie led the way to where Josiah sat on the edge of his bed. Max wondered how such a frail man was still alive. His blood boiled at the bruising around the old man's wrists and eyes.

The loud roar of a two-cylinder motor gunned to top-speed rent the air around them.

"What's that?" Max asked.

"My snowmobile." Josiah tried to rise, accepted Max's arm for support. "I keep one for emergencies. But it has a bad piston. I doubt he'll get far."

"Neither will we. He's lit another fire. And we're locked in." Callie's eyes met Max's.

He saw defeat crowding in, discoloring the rich blue irises. In all the time he'd known her, he'd never seen her so look so beat. Her gaze rested on his chest, the stain of red spreading over it.

"I'm sorry I got you into this, Max. I got you shot when I should never have allowed you to stay."

"Callie—"

"It's getting smoky. Can you help me find my coat and boots?" Josiah's request broke the chasm of unspoken words that lay between them.

"The cabin's on fire, Josiah. And there's no way out. The window's too small for any of us, and the door is blocked. I'm sorry. I should have done better."

What she didn't say was that they were all going to burn to death.

She'd failed.

Not only hadn't she achieved Josiah's signature for

Finders, she'd endangered Max in the process. Two innocents were going to die because she hadn't done her job.

Oh, God, why don't You help me?

"There's a way out. But I need my coat." Josiah's soft croak broke through her prayer.

"I'll get it." Max left, returned a few minutes later with the thick sheepskin coat, a knitted toque, heavy mitts and Callie's backpack. "Here you go."

They helped Josiah dress. Max pulled on one of the old man's quilted flannel shirts, insisted Callie don one, too. By now the cabin was full of smoke. Even with the bedroom door shut tight and bedding stuffed along the bottom it was hard to breathe.

"We have to get out of here before the beams start falling," she murmured.

"Pull the bed out," Josiah directed, wheezing with the effort of speech. He was leaning heavily on Max now.

Callie pulled, saw the small panel cut into the wall.

"Pull the chain. It will lift and we can crawl out," he said, his voice hoarse. "It's my fire escape."

"Josiah Harpnell, you are a wonder," Max breathed. "Callie, you go first."

She wanted to argue but then realized that he was going to have Josiah go next. Between them, they'd have to pull the old man through because he was growing weaker by the moment.

Finally they were all three outside but the snow and icy wind rapidly covered the ground in a soft layer. Would they now freeze to death?

"Wait." Josiah motioned to Callie. "Reach in to the left. There's a small leather pouch."

She found it, scrambled back out. Inside was a portable radio.

"If we can get to the top of the ridge, we can call for help on it. Whatever he gave me is making things spin." Josiah leaned back against a tree, closed his eyes.

"We need to get you out of here. Is there anything we could use? Another snowmobile?" she asked hopefully.

He shook his head. Then his eyes opened wide.

"The shed," he whispered. My dogsled is in the shed. I could lie on it if you could pull it."

"I'll get it." Callie edged around the side of the building. Terhan was gone, but just in case—she paused, then hurried forward. The cabin was burning higher and faster now, but because the shed was surrounded in corrugated metal, it had not caught. But the heat it radiated was intense.

Callie kicked at the door, took a breath and stepped inside. She saw a mound of furs, then finally the end of the sled.

"Way to go, Josiah," she murmured, tugging at the sled. It wouldn't move an inch. The heat in the shed was crushing the breath out of her. "Come on," she groaned.

"Here, I'll get behind it." Max moved past her. "On the count of three."

"What about your shoulder?"

"It's fine. One. Two. Three."

It took four tries but finally they got the sled and its furs out. It slid easily over the snow-frozen ground.

"I thought he'd stay warm if we wrapped him in the furs," she told Max, desperately wondering why he didn't ask her about the pictures, about the past.

"Good. We might all need them if we have to camp

out tonight. I don't think this storm is going to blow over too quickly."

They worked together to get the old man into the sled and covered with the warm fur pelts. He was feverish again, talking about the papers he'd signed.

"What if Terhan gets those papers filed before we get back?" Max asked in a soft voice.

"Don't worry," she reassured him. "The ones I gave Terhan won't work. That mark I made is a signal I have with Finders that the signatures aren't right. If Josiah can hang on, he can sign new ones when we get back to Victoria."

Josiah didn't hear her. He'd fallen asleep. Or he was unconscious.

In the bag with the radio Josiah had included a map clearly marked with the cabin's location and directions overland to the nearest forest ranger's station. Callie studied these while Max retrieved his pack from the base of the tree where he'd been shot. She wanted to ask about his shoulder but knew her query would be met with the same stoic response he'd given before.

She watched him walk back toward her. He was hurting and she knew it. But he never said a word.

"Isn't it farther to go there than back?" Max peered over her shoulder.

Callie studied the distances while her mind automatically noted his flat tone. He wasn't going to ask about the pictures, she knew that now.

"I think it's better if we go on. If we can't reach anyone with Josiah's radio, we'll at least be able to find shelter, maybe a radio at the ranger's. Besides, we could never pull Josiah back over that terrain. It'll be easier to use the clear-cuts to get there."

"Fine."

A quiet desperation filled her at the resignation in his voice. It was all over. Everything they'd shared had been shattered because of those pictures and with them any flicker of hope that his profession of love would be enough to withstand her past secrets.

It hadn't, of course. Nothing could.

And now it lay between them—a huge unspoken barrier.

As they trudged along through the biting wind, slipped and slid on icy snowflakes now covering the ground in a sheet of white, Callie knew filing for divorce had been the right thing to do. Some things were unforgivable and when Max saw the rest of those pictures he'd never want to see her again. Why hadn't he left the backpack behind—to burn?

For a moment she'd almost believed that God was there, that He heard her desperate prayer in the cabin.

Now she knew better.

They were alone out here, in the middle of a snowstorm with no food and no shelter. It would take a long time to reach the ranger's cabin; they'd have to camp out tonight.

Worse, though she hadn't told Max yet, she'd spotted snowmobile tracks running in a parallel course to theirs.

Which meant that if the snowmobile broke down, they'd probably run into Terhan.

Sooner or later.

TWELVE

"It's getting worse."

Callie didn't need the confirmation. Their cave/thicket provided protection from the icy wind and some of the snow, but the howl of a full-scale blizzard was too loud to miss.

"How's Josiah?"

She picked up the tin cup filled with warm water and stepped past the fire to check on the old man. Though he allowed a few drops of the liquid to dribble past his lips, he did not stir.

Callie touched his forehead.

"He's still too hot. I don't think the pills are doing anything." They'd found two headache tablets at the bottom of Max's sack. Callie had crushed one into the water, but had to feed it so slowly she was afraid Josiah was gaining little of the benefits.

"Maybe we've left on too many furs?"

"I don't think so."

They had removed a few pelts from the pile to cover themselves, but Josiah was still cozily wrapped in many of them. In one of his ramblings he'd told her he bought the skins from a native Canadian who killed only the weakened animals that could not otherwise survive the harsh climate. The money he got for the pelts he used to feed flocks of birds around his Yukon home.

When she'd done all she could for Josiah, Callie returned to her seat on the thick bearskin and lifted the end of another to shield herself from the cold.

"Will you tell me about your father, Callie?"

She'd known it was coming. Max had been too silent for too long. Now there was no place to go, no place to hide, no way to avoid his questions. She took a deep breath.

"My father was an ambassador. He and my mother loved the life, I didn't. We quarreled a lot. I was thirteen when we moved back to America. I hated our new life. I ran away from home. That's how I met Terhan." She so did not want to go there but it had to be said.

"The arguments got a lot worse, things degenerated between us. My parents were mortified by me." She bit the sentences off as quickly as she could, hoping it would be fast enough to stop any questions. "After my mother died, my father wanted nothing more to do with me. The day he accepted another posting we argued worse than ever before. He told me I could leave and not come back. So I did."

"Until Iraq."

"He was there. I thought maybe it was time to mend fences. He didn't." She could see he was trying to work it out, which was the last thing she wanted. "Do you want to take first watch or second?"

"Watch?" His eyebrows rose. "For what?"

"Animals. Terhan. I saw his tracks earlier. We might run into him."

His face tightened, his eyes narrowed. "Go to sleep, Callie. I'll watch."

It wasn't easy to rest. The wind whistled around so that every time she was almost comfortable, it snuck in a new corner. But her body was tired. And Callie knew she had to rest now. If Max's shoulder got any worse…

He was in a lot of pain. He'd refused the headache tablet, insisted she use it for Josiah. Callie had considered slipping it to him in his tea but decided to wait. If worse came to worst, she'd have to choose between Josiah and Max.

She could only pray it didn't come to that.

But then God didn't hear her prayers, did he?

Max eased forward gingerly, checked on Josiah then tossed another couple of branches onto the fire. He walked to the edge of their thicket, peered through the cedar boughs.

The wind was dying down. If the snow stopped they'd be able to make fairly good time tomorrow. Unless it started thawing. Josiah's sled wouldn't slide on mud. He walked back, huddled beside the fire.

What had Callie done? Any why hadn't she told him? The questions raged inside his brain. Pictures, Terhan had said. That she posed for pictures. Callie said she'd run away from home at thirteen, that she'd met Terhan then.

What kind of pictures could a thirteen-year-old girl have posed for?

He rejected the ugly images his brain concocted.

What about her father? Her dead father. That was another secret she'd kept. Why?

With every step they'd taken over the white terrain,

he'd tamped down the anger, telling himself he didn't know the whole story, that he shouldn't judge.

But he was her husband and he knew nothing of her past life—nothing she hadn't wanted him to know anyway.

Why, God? Why couldn't she have told me? And why does she keep pushing me away?

He pulled out the Testament, fingered through the pages but nothing seemed to penetrate to that angry hurt spot in the depths of his heart. More frustrating—all afternoon an old memory verse had spun round his brain.

Judge not that you be not judged.

But he was the victim here. She'd gotten him into this mess without letting him know what was really going on. She'd deliberately kept the truth hidden, even now she hadn't told all, he was sure of it. How could a marriage exist in that atmosphere?

Yes, God hated divorce. But didn't He also hate lies and deceit and keeping secrets from the person who trusted you most. All this time he'd given her the benefit of the doubt, believed that she just needed time to let him past her guard. But she'd had plenty of time and still Callie wasn't telling him everything.

Judge not.

The anger built, grew hotter than the pain flaming in his shoulder.

"I'm the victim here, God. That baby was mine, too. But I'm the one who found out last that I wasn't going to be a father."

Maybe she hadn't told him the complete truth about that, either. Maybe their child hadn't died but had been—No! The idea that Callie would have deliberately gotten rid of their baby was untenable.

But the suspicion had been planted. And the longer he watched her sleep, the harder that little nugget of suspicion buried inside him became. He saw her backpack lying by Josiah. The pictures were inside. The evidence of her lies and secrets.

He moved without thinking. Grasping the envelope he shoved it into his own pack and zipped it shut, suppressing the guilt.

I deserve to finally know the truth. How many times should I forgive? Seven times seven?

I say seventy times seven, Jesus replied.

"I can't forgive. Not anymore."

"Max? Who are you talking to?"

He blinked, saw Callie staring at him. "It doesn't matter."

She shed the bearskin, moved beside him and touched his forehead. "You're hot," she whispered. "You've got a fever."

"I'm fine." He knocked away her hand, moved to cover himself with the rug. "You can take over now."

"Fine." She said nothing more, didn't even look at him. Callie had never been stupid. She knew exactly what he wasn't saying.

Fine. Let her know. Max ignored the soft rebuke from his heart. It was time to cut himself free from her. Past time. The secrets had gone on for too long. Even now, out here, she couldn't come clean.

Well, he was done with asking. There came a time when a man had to hang on to what little pride he had left.

This was that time.

The walk up the ridge to the ranger station was grueling even though the blizzard had blown itself out. Callie tried to assume as much of the strain of dragging the sled uphill as she could, hoping to spare Max more pain.

He did not look well.

She kept checking his color surreptitiously, finding reasons for them to slow down, or stop altogether. But she didn't say a word. After three times refusing the one pill she had left, he had ordered her to stop asking. His voice brooked no argument.

The sky was pitch-black by the time they reached the cabin. The moon cast a beacon of light as they dragged Josiah the last fifty yards. Callie had tried the phone several times only to receive a No Service signal. The radio, filled with static, was little different. For now she ignored both, concentrated on simply getting the two men inside.

Ten feet from the building Max collapsed on the ground, his face white. Callie raced up to him, checked his pulse and found only a thread. She lifted the coat he wore, gasped at the amount of blood drenching the inside of his waterproof gear. If she didn't get help soon, he'd bleed to death.

She checked the door of the building. Locked. Using her gun now would send an echo all through the valley. If Terhan was out there, he'd know they hadn't died. She hadn't seen any tracks this morning, had no idea whether he'd veered off down through the pass or was somewhere parallel to them.

It didn't matter. She had two very sick men. They had to find shelter tonight or risk dying out here. Not to mention wild animals who would be attracted by the blood.

She aimed the gun at the lock and pulled the trigger.

Max seemed to wake up at the sound. He tried to rise. "He'll hear it."

"Doesn't matter. We've got to get out of the cold." She had no idea what the temperature was, only that the snow was not melting. "Come on, Max. Put your arm around me. I can't carry you and I'm afraid to drag you."

"Josiah first."

She refused to obey. "You first. Josiah is warm under those furs. You're not. Now come on. We're wasting time. I'm not letting you die out here, not after all of this. Let's go."

She moved to his good side, flung an arm around his waist and pulled. He managed to lift his uninjured arm and lay it across her shoulders but groaned as he struggled to move forward.

"Almost there," she encouraged. "Come on. You can do it."

"Forget it," he gasped, whitening with the effort until she thought he'd pass out. "I can't do it. It's too far. Give me a fur and I'll sleep out here. I'll be fine."

"Not a chance. Now move. What are you, a quitter?" Deliberately she goaded him, hoping he'd get mad and try harder. "You big tough he-men always crumble when the going gets tough. It's always the same," she huffed, forcing herself to move forward.

"Shut up," he mumbled, his face caved in lines of strain so deep sweat poured off his face.

"I don't think so, fella. Not while I'm the one doing all the work." *Come on, Max, just a little farther, my darling.* "If I'd known I'd have to save your backside I'd have asked for hazard pay."

He grunted but stepped through the door, grabbed it for support. "What about Josiah?"

Callie had no idea how she'd get the other man inside. She'd exhausted her strength manhandling Max.

"Don't worry about him. Let's get you over on that cot. Easy now." She struggled to hold him as he almost collapsed onto the cot. "Just stay there and rest. I'll be back."

Every muscle in her body protested at the thought but she walked back outside, refusing to give up. As long as she could move, neither of these men would die.

"Please God, help us."

No answer.

She studied the sled from every angle. If she'd had a rope she could have worked out some kind of winch to pull it the last bit, but without that—there was no way she could budge the sled.

"Is everything all right?" The voice emerged little more than a sqeaking whisper but when Callie drew away the thick covering, brown eyes looked back at her with a clarity she welcomed.

"How are you feeling?"

"Surprisingly well. I think the worst of whatever he gave me has worked its way through my system." He pushed away the fur, sat up and glanced around. "We're at the ranger's station," he murmured.

"Yes. Can you get inside if I help you?" she asked, half-afraid to hear the answer.

"I'm sure I can. There's a walking stick attached to the side. Perhaps you could give me that."

She found it, worked it free and handed it to him after she'd pushed away the coverings.

"If you sat on the fur I could drag that to the cabin," she murmured.

He glanced at her, smiled, then slowly, very carefully eased himself from the sled using the stick to stand upright.

"I don't think that will be necessary, but thank you." He found his footing, then held out one arm. "If you could assist me, though, I'd be most appreciative."

She had to smile at his formal manners. They were in the back of beyond but he was so polite.

"There was a man with you," he murmured as they slowly moved forward.

"My husband, Max. He's inside. Terhan shot him and he's bleeding pretty badly." *But he's not going to die, God. Don't You dare take him!*

"The station usually has a first aid kit. I have a small amount of training. We should be able to stop the bleeding."

"Are you all right?" she asked when they'd gone halfway.

"My dear, I generally trek about a thousand miles a summer. I assure you I'm much tougher than I look. It was that man's drugs that knocked me for a loop. He kept pumping them into me."

Josiah moved steadily forward until they were inside.

"Oh, my," he murmured, glancing at Max. "Perhaps you could bring the furs. We don't want him going into shock."

Perfectly happy to have someone else take over for a few moments, Callie made three trips to bring everything inside. She pushed the empty sleigh around to the back of the building behind some trees. No telling if they'd need it again.

By the time she returned inside, Josiah had a fire going with some of the wood from a wood box pushed against the wall. A kettle sat atop the cookstove.

"There's a stream that comes out of the mountains about two hundred meters uphill toward the tower. Could you get some water?" he asked, one eyebrow raised. "I've already put in what you had left in the bottle but I'll need more for him."

"Okay." Struggling upright from the hand-hewn chair Callie grabbed the small pail hanging on a nail and went back outside. She climbed slowly, organizing her thoughts.

First the water. Then she'd go back up the hill and try Max's cell phone from there. Surely she'd be able to get through up there?

Access to the stream was tricky. Since it was autumn, runoff from the snowcap had diminished. The rocks along the edge gleamed slick in the moonlight with melted snow now frozen into a thin skin of ice. Callie slipped twice, soaking her left foot up to her calf. She gritted her teeth against the icy numbness and filled the pail as quickly as possible. By the time she returned to the cabin she was freezing.

Josiah was sitting beside Max, trying to feed him something.

"What's that?"

"The rangers always keep a few food supplies here in case someone gets stranded. I found some dried soup packets. He needs liquids."

Max's face wore a sheen of sweat. Every so often his head thrashed from one side to the other as if he were enduring some horrible nightmare.

"The infection's getting worse. That bullet has to come out."

Callie stared. "You know how to do that?"

"I've never done it before, if that's what you're asking," Josiah said as he sponged off Max's face. "But what's the alternative? He'll die if we don't do something. Please put that water on to boil."

Shocked into silence Callie obeyed, only realizing as she dumped one cupful after another into the kettle that the room was warm. Her sneaker thawed, squelched with every step she took, but she ignored it.

She had to get help. Max could not, would not die. She couldn't be responsible for another death.

"Are you queasy?" Josiah's dark eyes studied her. "This isn't going to be pretty and I need to know if you'll be passing out."

"I'll be fine," she told him, gritting her teeth when he nodded, then slowly removed Max's bloody shirt.

"Bring the lantern over here."

She hadn't even noticed the source of light. Callie grasped the small kerosene lamp and moved it to a stand just a few inches above Max's head. She followed Josiah's directions, easing one shoulder free of the shirt, using her knife to tear the rest away.

"Max had some headache pills. We fed you one, but I still have one left. Do you want it for him?"

"Later." Josiah's fingers gently probed the wound.

As if sensing that watching was like having her own heart ripped out, he kept speaking, giving her jobs to do.

"The water should be hot now. Pour some into the pail. Find some kind of cloth. And bring me that first aid kit off the wall."

Callie said nothing, simply did his bidding. It seemed to her that Max was weakening, that he was fighting less and less.

He could die.

The words hammered into her heart, crushing everything but the need to help him.

"Please God, please let him be okay," she whispered to herself over and over, like a mantra. "Come on, darling. Fight."

"There's antiseptic of some kind, right? Alcohol, something?"

"There are swabs," she told him. "Nothing liquid."

"Open some. But wash your hands in the basin first."

Callie obeyed. When she returned to his side, the blood had been wiped away. The hole in Max's shoulder was small but lethal-looking.

"Is he asleep?" she whispered.

"Passed out. Just as well. I have nothing to give him for the pain." He pressed lightly on the area around the wound. "Check the first aid kit. Are there tweezers?"

"No."

"Then look around for a knife, pinchers, something I can use as an instrument."

"Max had a knife." She scrounged in his backpack. Her hand froze when she encountered the brown envelope. He'd taken the pictures.

"Did you find it?"

"Yes." Her fingers closed around the army knife, pulled it free. She handed it over, watched him wipe it with the antiseptic swabs. But her eyes kept straying back to that envelope.

She could take it, burn it. Then he'd never see them. They'd be destroyed forever.

Or until Terhan had another set printed.

The truth hit her between the eyes. She would never be free of the past. No matter what she did, it was there, lodged in her head. She'd tried so hard, struggled for so long to keep it under wraps, to hide it beneath the busyness of work. All these years she'd pretended that mistake was someone else's.

But it was hers.

Let Max look at the pictures. What did it matter? Nothing could hurt more than the look in his eyes after Terhan's exposé.

"Callie!"

She turned, stared at Josiah. "Yes?"

"I need help."

She moved to stand beside him. "What do you want me to do?"

"Put your hand here and hold it still. I've found the bullet, I just need to get it out." He began to probe.

Bright red blood oozed out, trickled across Max's tanned chest like an arrow aiming for his heart.

She grabbed a handful of gauze and gently wiped the red stain away, gritting her teeth when it didn't stop. She kept her mouth closed but mentally she begged Josiah to hurry.

After many tense minutes he finally lifted his hand away.

"I've got it."

Callie took the bullet from him, wrapped it in a bit of cloth she tore from Max's shirt. The police would want it later. She tucked the bullet into her backpack, then changed the water in the pail, tossing the red-stained water out onto the snow before replacing it with fresh hot water. How she wished she hadn't left her painkillers on the boat.

Josiah worked quickly, cleansing the wound with tedious precision. Then he covered it with a fresh pad of gauze and taped that in place. Satisfied with his work he lifted the small gray blanket that had been on the cot and laid it over Max.

"If you can crush that pill now, we can give it to him. It might dull the edge of the pain when he wakes up."

"When will that be?"

"I don't know." Josiah touched his forehead. "He's lost a lot of blood, Callie. His breathing isn't strong. I'd guess he was close to hypothermic when we got here. He needs to be in the hospital."

The call!

She'd forgotten all about making that call.

Callie grabbed her jacket, pulled it on. She found her gloves, dragged her backpack near and took out the radios she'd recovered from Josiah's cabin.

"I tried these before and couldn't get them to work. They're different than any I've used before. Am I doing something wrong?"

He showed her the features, how to change frequencies.

"I replaced the batteries recently so they should work," Josiah said. He studied her face. "Are you sure it's safe to go up the mountain?"

"No. But it's no safer to sit here and we need help. I have to at least try." She removed her gun from its ankle holster. "You know to shoot, don't you, Josiah?"

He nodded, but a cloud lingered in the back of his eyes. "I don't like weapons very much."

"Trust me, neither do I. But we both know Terhan isn't averse to using force. If he happens to come here, I want you to shoot him, in the leg or something. Render him incapable, do you understand?"

"But—"

"No buts. Listen to me, Josiah. Terhan killed Aaron. He tried to kill Max and he wants your inheritance. He's not going to simply forget about it." She glanced at Max. "I should have shot him earlier but I couldn't get a clear shot."

The guilt billowed up inside. So many things she'd done wrong. But she couldn't focus on that now.

"That's my husband lying there, Josiah. Max did nothing to Terhan, yet he might lose his life because of him. I want you to make sure that Terhan doesn't get to Max again. Do you understand me?"

Josiah nodded, eyes clear. "I'm sorry about Aaron. He was a troubled man."

You don't know the half of it, she wanted to say. But Callie kept silent, watching him. Finally his shoulders went back, his head lifted.

"I'll make sure nothing happens to Max, Callie."

"Thank you." She laid the gun in the palm of his hand. "Do you know how to use this one?"

He glanced at it. "Yes."

"Good. Keep it tucked in the back of your waistband so it's handy. I'll be back as soon as I can." She zipped up her jacket, headed for the door.

"Callie?"

The whispered word came from the man lying on the bed.

"I'm here, Max." She knelt by his bed.

"Where are you going?" he croaked, his voice husky.

"To get help. Josiah's going to stay with you. He got the bullet out but you lost a lot of blood. You have to rest." She couldn't resist reaching out to brush away the hank of hair that threatened to tumble over one eye. "There's a tower at the top of the mountain. I'll climb up there. I should be able to reach someone from that location."

"Be careful," he whispered. Then he closed his eyes.

"I will." She touched his cheek, let her palm cradle it, willing her strength into him. "I'm sorry, Max. I'm so sorry. About all of it. I wish—"

What was the point of wishing? She lifted her hand away, rose but she could not move away.

She loved this man, more than she'd ever loved anyone in her life. No matter how many missions she'd taken, how many dangers she'd been through, Max was home base, her safety net, the one who'd always been there for her.

But he wouldn't be anymore.

She leaned down, brushed her lips against his.

"Goodbye, Max. I love you."

Turning she walked out the door, closed it softly behind her.

The night was hushed except for the crackle of her feet on the ice-crusted snow. The night air was crisp, cold, her breath clouds of mist in the frosty atmosphere. Winter wasn't far away.

Callie used the moonlight to choose her path, carefully picking her way around boulders and patches of vegetation glistening like silver. She couldn't risk slipping, not when Max's life depended on her getting help. Her wet foot had gone numb after the first ten or fifteen minutes but she ignored that, kept pressing upward.

Ahead, above the jagged crest of the mountains, diamond glints grew visible as constellation patterns in the northern sky. Only once before had she seen them sparkle so brightly, on a camping trip with Max. The two of them had sprawled in their sleeping bags on a midsummer's night and watched a meteor shower. Later, much later, he'd woken her to show her the stars.

"My dad used to tell me the night sky was God's carpet," he'd whispered. "One tailor-made for Heaven. See the Big Dipper. That's what God drinks from. The Little Dipper's for the angels. And there, Orion's Belt. That's what God wore when he went into battle to help the Israelites."

Max had spun a pretty tale, made God seem personal, intimate, someone she could trust. And for a while Callie had believed him.

Until God turned His back on her.

Or had He?

Funny how tonight she could almost sense that same closeness she'd felt so long ago.

"Are You there? Can You help me?" she whispered, then called herself an idiot. God had better things to do that fix her mistakes.

But the higher she went, the stronger her impression that she was not alone, that Someone was very near, waiting.

Finally she reached the summit. She pulled out the radios, turned them on the way Josiah had told her and began her call for help. Nothing but static. She repeated it twice, three times.

Nothing.

Frustrated, she set them aside, pulled out Max's cell phone and turned it on. It seemed to take forever for the thing to boot up. Would there be enough battery power left to send a call?

A very small amount of the power bar showed. If this call didn't work, the phone would be useless. She held it up, waiting.

No signal.

Her heart sank. There were no other options.

Okay, maybe one.

Either you reach out and grab it with both hands, accept it. Or you decide it isn't for you, that you're the exception, and you let it go. It's your choice.

Callie was going to grab.

"Please God, we need help. Max needs help. I'm not asking for me. It doesn't matter about me. But it matters about Max. He believes in You. He trusts You. Please help."

Turn around.

So certain was she that someone had spoken Callie glanced over one shoulder. There was no one there.

Turn around. Face west.

She turned, held up her cell phone. The signal was there.

"Thank you. Thank you."

She dialed Finders Inc., the SOS number. A voice answered.

"This is Callie Merton. I need help. Max is wounded, I have Josiah Harpnell with me. I'm at a ranger's station in the Yukon but I can't give you an exact location. You'll have to triangulate from this signal. We need a chopper. Immediately. It's life or death."

She tried to think of anything else pertinent but in that moment of hesitation the signal was gone and she was again in a No Service area. A moment later the phone went black. Dead battery.

Callie closed the phone, slipped it into her pocket, a sense of wonderment filling her heart.

Had that been God?

She didn't know. She could only gaze into the night sky as a star tumbled from high above, leaving a tail of light behind it.

It seemed incredulous to believe that God would send His answer to her prayer in that way, but how else to explain what had just happened?

With the message delivered, she turned, picked up the radios and began to descend the mountain. She'd gone only a hundred feet when a dark shadow appeared in front of her, creeping down the same trail she'd climbed up such a short while ago.

Terror filled her when she recognized Terhan and the rifle in his hand. She had to do something. If he found Max and Josiah alive inside that cabin, he'd kill them both.

Callie stuffed the radio in her pocket, crept forward as quickly as she dared, following him as she tried to come up with a plan. She had no gun, nothing to protect herself. But she would die before she let him get to Max.

Terhan slinked over the switchback trail below her. In a few seconds he would be directly beneath her. She had the element of surprise but only if she acted immediately.

You have to choose, Callie. Either you believe in God

or you don't. If you believe, you have to trust that He will be there for you.

I believe in You, God, she prayed silently. *I'm sorry I didn't understand that You were always there. Please help me now. Please.*

Then she crouched down, waited for exactly the right moment and launched herself onto the killer lurking below.

Terhan's rifle went off, he tumbled beneath her, issued one horrible curse, then was silent.

In that instant Callie saw the stars above her go out.

THIRTEEN

Warm hands touched his arm. Something pierced his skin—a needle. Then warm blankets were snuggled around him.

"We're taking you out now. Try to stay still, Max."

That voice—Daniel?

Max forced his eyes open, stared at his best friend. His lips weren't working and he couldn't make them speak until they lifted him onto a stretcher. The shock of pain from being moved jerked the words out from his parched throat.

"How did—?"

"Callie called us. We tracked your cell phone from the towers." Daniel said something to two other men who lifted his stretcher and began carrying him outside.

"Wait!"

They stopped, Daniel moved beside him. "What is it?"

"Where is Callie?"

"We don't know yet, Max."

Max had never seen Daniel as worried as he looked at this moment. Something was very wrong.

"We can't find her. I sent a man up the trail to the tower but she wasn't there. The terrain's too rough to search very far off the trail in the dark but don't worry. We're not leaving until we find her. In the meantime, you and Josiah need to go to the hospital. The chopper will take you."

He nodded to the attendants but Max grabbed his arm and held on, preventing them from moving him.

Daniel sighed. "What is it, Max?"

"Terhan. He could still be out there."

"I know. Is this yours?" Daniel held up his backpack.

Max saw the corner of the envelope sticking out and remembered the pictures. If the police came here they'd poke through everything. Better to remove them with him.

"Yes." He patted the stretcher beside him. "I want it."

Daniel set the bag at his side. His surprised expression was soon masked. "Time to go, buddy. You're going to be fine."

"You find her, Daniel," Max ordered, his fingers closing around the damning evidence as his eyes met the other man's in an unspoken communication. "You don't leave here till you find Callie."

"We won't." Daniel's speculative gaze rested on him for several moments. "You might do some praying while you're waiting. This is the wilderness. Anything can happen."

"I haven't stopped praying since we started out on this trip," Max assured him. "Let me know?"

"As soon as I do."

Max nodded, allowed them to carry him to the chopper. He should have walked but for some reason his body didn't seem to want to obey him. Everything was a haze of pain that grew into a cloud of unreality. The shot, he supposed. He knew from a past boating accident that morphine had a way of altering his perceptions.

As the chopper lifted off and carried him to safety, Max shifted, felt the crackle of the envelope under his hand.

How could she have done this thing? he asked himself for the hundredth time. How could she have kept it from him all this time?

His alter ego, his conscience, a voice inside his head—someone—debated him.

Because you would have judged her, just as you're judging her now.

"I've never judged her."

You judge her all the time. Even now you're wondering if she reacted fast enough, if she allowed Terhan to get to her.

"I don't do that."

The truth is hard to face.

"What truth?"

You spouted a lot of stuff to her about trusting God, depending on Him, leaning on Him. But you don't do that with her.

"Yes, I do."

No. You believe God's with you, caring for you. But you don't really believe the same for her. That's why you've tried so hard to make her fit into your mold.

"I haven't done that!"

What about the baby? What about when she told you it was gone—your first reaction was to judge her for not taking enough care, for risking his life in something you thought foolish, even dangerous. But maybe it wasn't only her. Maybe God had a reason for allowing David's death that you can't figure out.

"What reason?"

You see, even now you can't trust that God has His own plans for Callie and He hasn't consulted with you. You say you trust Him, can't you trust Him with Callie, believe that He's watching over her, protecting her far better than you ever could? Or have?

"But I'm the one who was wronged! I'm the one she's kept—is keeping secrets from."

Judge not that you be not judged.

"I haven't hidden anything."

Of course you have. We all do. Look inside. Deeper. Do you see the fear hiding there? You try to control her because you're afraid.

"No!"

You say you want truth, honesty. Look inside yourself, Max. That's fear you're hiding, fear that something will happen, that one day she won't come back and you'll be hurt. Fear is what has kept you apart as much as any secrets. It's your fear that keeps driving her away.

"How?"

Callie can't be honest with you because you don't want her, you want the woman who fits your mold. Callie isn't the only one keeping secrets, Max. You've kept a horrible one of your own.

There was another voice, two of them. They came from above him not inside him. Max struggled to stay awake, to understand what they were saying.

"Who's he talking to?"

"Himself, I guess. Must be a reaction to the shot. He's fighting it, but my guess is another few minutes and he'll be out cold."

Max felt a rush of sympathy for this other man. He

was wide awake and intent on praying for Callie's safety. He closed his eyes.

"He's out."

She was cold, so cold. And aching.

Callie curled in the fetal position, trying to find some warmth. Pain shot up from her wrist and she heard herself mewl a cry.

Noise. Something was happening. She tried to see down the hillside but a bush blocked her view. Moments later an icy brush of arctic air rushed over her as rotor blades carried a chopper up and away.

They must have picked up Max and Josiah.

"Thank you, God." At least he'd be safe. That's what she prayed for.

Callie closed her eyes, too worn out to hold them open anymore. The sounds down the hill had quieted now. There was nothing but peace and the soft cadence of rushing water somewhere nearby.

"I'll be seeing you soon, baby," she murmured, gazing up into the stars. "It won't be long and Mama will be there with you."

She had no fear. Max had said God would be with her; she understood now that He was there, that He'd always been there. Beneath her the radio issued a static scratch that disturbed her dream. She pushed it away, fought to recover the sweet sense of acceptance that she was finished now.

She shifted, stared upward at the sky. "I'm ready, God."

A noise disturbed her. She twisted her head.

"You will not ruin this for me, Callie." Terhan loomed over her, the barrel of his rifle pointed at her head. "You ruined my life once, you're not going to do it again."

Callie had only one thought—for Max.

"Please let him forgive me," she whispered.

The sound of gunshot shattered the night.

It was over.

"Daniel here."

"It's Max."

Silence.

"Don't bother trying to put me off, Daniel. I want to know where she is."

"I told you that we found her, Max."

"And?"

They'd told him something but he'd been on pain-killers at the time and much of that night and the following days were still blurry. He'd even imagined Callie had visited him once, though the nurse had denied that.

"We tracked Callie through a radio she was carrying. I shot Terhan. He had her in point-blank range and he refused to put his gun down. Callie was air lifted, taken to hospital, treated and released. Once she'd given her statement to police we told her to take some time off. She's not here at Finders."

"Then where is she? I checked her place. No one's seen her. The super's looking after her mail but he doesn't know where she went or when she'll return. Even Lisa doesn't know."

"Is it urgent that you talk to her? Your mother—"

"Is fine. She's finished the chemo and doing well. Thanks for asking."

"Then?"

"Callie's my wife, Daniel."

"Was."

A bolt of fear shafted its way to his heart, chasing away everything else. "What do you know?" he asked hoarsely.

"I don't *know* anything, Max," Daniel told him. "Callie keeps everything bottled inside. She'd hardly confide her personal decisions to me. All I know is that she said she was refiling the divorce papers and she asked for some time away."

"So?"

Daniel's heavy sigh needed no translation.

"Look, buddy. When we got to her she was suffering from hypothermia. When she was released she asked for time to recuperate and we gave her time off with the understanding that we wouldn't call her in unless something urgent came up. It hasn't. I have no idea where she is or what she's doing."

"Then call her in. I need to talk to her." Frustration nipped at him sharpening his voice.

"No can do."

"Name one good reason why not."

"Because she needs a break. She wasn't lost, Max. And she wasn't too hurt to move. She knew exactly how to get back to the cabin. But she didn't even try to go there. Do you know why?"

"No."

Daniel's voice hardened to a harsh, biting tone.

"Because she was afraid Terhan would follow her and kill you. So she huddled down on that frozen ground and kept silent. Do you realize what that means?"

The mental picture Daniel had just drawn stunned him. Max couldn't speak.

"She was willing to give up her life to save yours."

Daniel paused, let the silence stretch between them. "She must love you a great deal to do that," he whispered.

"Enough to divorce me?" The ignominy of it burned deeply. "I got more papers this morning. She wants to proceed immediately. What kind of love is that?"

"You tell me, buddy."

There was nothing to say to that. Max hung up, slamming the phone into the cradle with a lot more force than necessary. His gaze rested on the divorce documents he'd just received, then went to the envelope beneath them. He hated that envelope but he couldn't seem to throw it away.

He glanced around the room, spotted the tiny porcelain doll she'd brought home from a mission in Japan, the gilt filagree egg from France, the lace cushions from Belgium. All part of her attempt to make this house her home, her refuge.

She's gone. And she's not coming back.

On top of that another voice, one he'd pushed to the back of his mind burst free and commanded his attention.

It's fear.

Max grasped the phone, hit redial.

"Daniel? Please, just listen to me, will you?"

FOURTEEN

"**M**ax?" Callie's fingers tightened around the cell phone, waiting ever so long before a hard, masculine voice finally answered.

"Yes."

"Don't hang up. Please?"

"Where are you?"

"At Finders Inc. In the boardroom. Shelby called me in. Something rush, she said. But that's not why I want to talk to you."

"Then why?"

"I promised I wouldn't leave town again without talking to you. So I called. But really I want to apologize. I should never have kept my past a secret from you."

Now he'd tell her he'd signed the papers.

"Why did you?"

"Isn't it obvious? I was ashamed." She swallowed. This was so hard.

But she had to apologize, she knew that. He wouldn't be able to forgive her but at least she'd leave knowing she'd been truthful.

"All those years ago, I ran away from home so sure I could show my parents I didn't need them, that I could take care of myself. I had no idea how hard it would be to get a job."

The memory of that horrible time was vivid in her mind, as if had happened yesterday, but she plowed on in a whisper.

"I slept in the park for three nights before Terhan found me. He offered me a place to stay. I was starving, soaked and more scared than I'd ever been, but I figured he couldn't be worse than the drunks I'd fought off the night before."

Such a long silence. Maybe he'd hung up.

"Are you there, Max?"

"Yes. Go on."

Go on? How could she say it, where would the words come from to explain what she'd done?

"Terhan was okay for two days. I did some laundry, cleaned up his place, cooked a couple of meals. He seemed happy with that. Until one night." Callie did not want to remember. But she had no choice. She'd told God she would tell the truth.

"What happened that night?"

"He brought this guy over, a creep. He had a look in his eyes, you know? Evil." She shuddered, forced herself to keep talking. "Terhan said the time had come for me to pay my debt. He said he got me some new clothes, that unless I posed for some pictures, I'd have to leave. Both of them were acting so weird. I knew something was wrong. So I left."

So much silence. She pressed on.

"I didn't get far. That night I ended up huddling under an overpass to hide from the pimp who wanted me to work for him."

Shame suffused her in a wave that stretched from head to toe. Why hadn't she gone home then? Why had she been so stubborn?

"I tried to keep it together for a couple more days but I had no money and someone stole my jacket,when I fell asleep. Terhan found me in a bus shelter, half-frozen, cowering from a crackhead with a knife. He got me out of there, let me sleep, then repeated his offer. I left again. Three times. Each time on the street was worse than the last. Finally I couldn't take it anymore, I was too scared. I put on the clothes, posed the way they said and let them take the pictures."

Bitter tears coursed down her cheeks. She wished he would say something but what, after all, could he say?

"It was horrible. I felt so dirty, so ugly. I was only thirteen but I knew those pictures were wrong." She scrubbed the tears from her cheeks, forced calm into her voice. She didn't want his sympathy. She didn't deserve it.

"As soon as they left the apartment to get the film developed, I stole the camera, hocked it for ten dollars and got out of there. I knew that I couldn't stay on the street anymore. Terhan would come after me, maybe want more pictures. No matter what, I had to go home."

The silence was killing.

Maybe he didn't care. Maybe he was just being polite.

"Keep talking, Callie."

"I stole some clothes, changed, cleaned myself up and hitchhiked my way home. I'd left a note to say I was going on a school trip. None of the staff had questioned it. My parents were away. I slipped back into my old life and they never even knew what happened. Life went on as normally as it ever had."

"Until?"

He wanted her to tell it all, to make her grovel? Well, she deserved that.

"Until I was sixteen. I was at a school dance one evening. Terhan saw me. He was coming down from a high, had the shakes. He needed a fix pretty badly."

This was the worst part, the part she hated to even think of, let alone talk about. But Max deserved to know it all. She owed him that. Then it would finally be over.

"He said that if I didn't get him some money he'd hurt me. All I had was what was left of my allowance money. I gave it to him thinking he'd disappear, leave me alone. I had no idea he'd followed me home. But he did. And then he did his research. Once he knew I was the daughter of an ambassador, he figured he'd hit the mother lode."

She had to stop, catch her breath and prepare for the worst.

"I'm still listening."

Callie squeezed her eyes tight, gulped. This was so hard.

"He blew everything I'd given to him and came back for more. When I said I didn't have any more, he phoned at all hours, threatened me. I met him to reason with him but he was really bad by then, shaking like a leaf and desperate to score some coke. He had the pictures, said if I didn't get him some cash fast he'd make sure my parents saw each and every portrait of their little girl all dressed up for company."

Max said nothing. In fact the silence was eerily tense, as if he couldn't wait for her to finish so he could hang up.

"I couldn't think what to do. Finally I stole a piece of my mother's jewelry and hocked it. When I got home that afternoon, it was late. Nobody seemed to be around. I went into the study, saw the pictures of me scattered across the floor. There was an envelope lying on the desk, addressed to my parents." She drew a shaky breath.

Would he understand?

"My mom valued her social position above everything, Max. She loved the prestige of being an ambassador's wife and she spent her life making sure that reputation wasn't tarnished, not by me, not by anyone. We argued so often about my disappointing them, ruining my dad's chances for promotion."

Sadness overwhelmed her that she'd never been the daughter they wanted but she refused to dwell on it.

Callie struggled to go on, to admit what she'd done.

"I was so afraid when I saw the pictures. I knew what they would do to her, how devastated she would be. I was right." She knuckled her eyes, refusing to stop the truth.

"I found her lying on her bed, an empty vial of sleeping pills on the floor. She'd killed herself. There was a note on the floor. It said the pictures were being sent to a magazine. The whole world was going to know the ambassador's daughter's secret unless Terhan got fifty thousand dollars."

A yawning gape stretched between phones. Callie had to finish. Then she never intended to speak of it again.

"My dad came home. He hid the pictures, took the note, called the coroner, paid Terhan, but he was like a zombie. During the funeral, after, he never spoke to me, not even once. It was as if I was dead, too. To him I was."

Bitter tears coursed down her cheeks at the memories.

"It took Terhan a while to blow through that much money. I was in college when the next threat came. After my mother's death, my father had dumped me in a boarding school, sold our house and moved to Europe. I never heard from him again, never got a birthday or Christmas card. I lived at the school year-round. When I was finished, the school told me they had money for my college tuition. I took my courses, graduated. The day of my graduation Terhan showed up again, he wanted more money. A lot more."

She forced a mantle of control over her emotions, chose a cool, firm tone to tell the rest.

"I wrote my father to ask what I should do. He sent my letter back, unopened. I knew then that I had to fix it myself or it would happen again and again. So I went to the police. We set up a sting, the pictures for money. Terhan was delighted, until he realized I'd betrayed him. I went to court, let them rake over every sordid detail so that he'd be convicted. Terhan sent someone to threaten me but it was too late for intimidation. He'd already ruined my life. I didn't think there was anything more he could do. I testified against him for blackmail, drug trafficking, a bunch of stuff I'd seen. He went to jail."

Such a long time ago. She got lost in the past, the mistakes, the wrong decisions. Callie blinked away the hurt.

"Your father never called you at all?" Max asked.

"No. Once the trial was over, my name was mud. Nobody wanted to hire me. I had no money, no work and no one to turn to. I left town, drove as far away as I could. I ended up in Victoria, alone, broke and desperate to eat. One day in the park I pretended I was canvassing for the needy and tried to get Daniel to donate. He bought my disguise and gave me a great donation but I felt so guilty I gave him back the money. He offered me a job. That's how I started with Finders Inc."

She swallowed, finding it hard to finish the story.

"I never heard from my father again. When I was in Paris on a mission, I found out he was living there and went to his house, tried to speak to him. He acted as if he didn't know me."

Her eyes stung as if she'd been stabbed by a red-hot poker. But Callie refused to cry, just as she always had.

"I know I deserved it. I know he hated me for what I'd caused. I know I had no right to expect him to forgive me. But I needed his forgiveness so badly. I just couldn't leave it alone. I decided to try one more time. I'd lost track of him so I used Finders to run a search. Eventually I learned he was negotiating in Iraq. I waited for a mission that would be nearby, grabbed at the opportunity when Finders needed a courier to Baghdad. It was the perfect opportunity. I had to make that last effort."

She paused, listened. Nothing, no sound. Just emptiness.

"Did you hear me, Max?"

"I heard."

She wished he'd say something else. But there was nothing to say, and she knew it.

"When I got there I learned he'd been ill, was near death. I went to the hospital to beg him to forgive me. For three days I sat at his bedside. Over and over I told him how sorry I was, that I'd never meant to hurt them. I told him about you, about the baby—that he was going to be a grandfather, about my work."

She'd lost her parents and she would lose Max, too. All because of one stupid mistake. Callie prayed for strength, felt a warm peace invade her heart. She told the rest of it as calmly as she could.

"He only spoke once. He told me to go away. That he was going to see his wife. Then he died. On my way back to the hotel I had the accident. And I lost the baby."

Still holding the phone, hoping, praying for some response, Callie walked to the window, stared out into the darkness and listened for some sign that Max understood.

When nothing came she rushed into speech.

"I'm sorry I never told you, Max. If I could, I'd go back to the first day we met and tell you all of it. Then you would have turned your back on me, that would have been better." She gripped the phone hard, forced the words out in spite of the pain.

"But I can't go back, Max. I can't undo anything. All I can say is that I'm deeply sorry you never got your son."

"So am I."

Behind her the door opened. Callie ignored it. She needed these last few minutes of privacy. Then she'd go back to doing her job.

"Go away," she said to whoever had just come in.

"I can't do that, Callie."

That voice—it wasn't just on the phone. She whirled around, stared at the doorway. Max stood there, his phone in one hand. He clicked it closed, his gaze locked on her.

"You're here. Why? Did Shelby call you?" She yearned to reach out, to touch his face, to beg him to understand. That was asking the impossible. "Is that why you've come?"

He closed the door. His head moved from side to side

and he walked steadily forward, pausing only when he stood directly in front of her.

"No."

"Then why?"

"Because I love you."

She stared, suspended in a bubble of disbelief. How could he? After all that had happened, after having his boat ruined, his life endangered, having lost his child because of her—how could he?

She sank onto a nearby chair, her legs unable to support her.

Max's hand reached out, took her phone and set it aside. Her throat closed as he knelt in front of her, his big powerful hands wrapping around hers.

"I came to ask your forgiveness. And to say I'm sorry."

Then she saw the tears in his eyes. "Sorry—for what?"

"That I wasn't there when you needed me most, that I doubted you. That you've carried this for so long by yourself."

"It was my mistake. I had to deal with it." She didn't trust what he was saying.

"It was the mistake of a kid whose parents should have been there for her, Cal." He let go of one hand, tossed an envelope on the table. "Those are pictures of a scared kid who ran away from home because nobody told her she was loved. That girl made a mistake, but she is not to be pitied."

"You kept them?" She stared at him, trying to understand.

"They're not mine to destroy. Terhan's dead. He will never bother you again. You're free of him."

"I know. But—"

"You faced the enemy, Cal. You faced him twice. You had the guts to stand up to him in court then and then you had the brains to stop him from hurting a helpless old man and me. At the risk of your own life. This girl—" he touched her cheek "—this *woman* is strong and beautiful and loved so much."

"You forgive me?" She could hardly believe it.

"Forgiveness isn't up to me, sweetheart. I wish you'd told me, I wish you'd let me help, but I'm not the one who needs to forgive you."

She frowned at him, not understanding.

"Have you asked God to forgive you?"

"Of course. Many times."

"Then you're forgiven from the only One who matters. He forgave you the very first time you asked." He touched her hair. "The problem is you have to accept that forgiveness. You keep beating yourself up for something that God doesn't even see anymore."

"But I lied to you."

"How about this—I'll forgive you if you'll forgive me."

"You?"

He nodded.

"For what?"

"You can even ask?" He touched her forehead, smoothed her eyebrows, trailed his fingers to her cheek. "So many things I wish I could do over, Cal. I shouldn't have pushed you to tell me something you wanted to bury. I let you think you weren't the most important person in my world. I failed to stand beside you when you needed me most. I let my sadness about the baby wash onto you when his death was not your fault."

"It didn't matter."

"Of course it did." He stared directly into her eyes. "I let my fear that one day you'd go and never come back crush my faith in God's plan for your life. I tried to take over when I should have given over. But I never once stopped loving you, Cal. Not ever."

"Oh, Max." She leaned forward, rested her head against his shoulder. "I thought you hated me."

"You can't hate a part of yourself. And you're part of me, Cal. The best part." He tilted her head up, touched her lips. "I don't want a divorce. I want a marriage. With you. Forever."

"Even if I stay with Finders Inc.?" she asked quietly.

"Your job is part of you, I know that now. Your work matters to the world. I'm proud of what you accomplish, of the way you can completely submerge yourself and become what you have to so you can get the answers you need." His gaze held her captive. "All I'm asking is that when you come home, you be Callie Merton Chambers, my wife, whom I love more than life."

"Are you sure, Max?" She touched his face, grazed the tip of her finger over his earlobe, dared to wrap her hand around the back of his neck. "Are you sure this is what you want? I'll have to take some assignments that you won't like, I may become someone you don't recognize."

"Not in here." He touched her heart. "I'll always recognize what's in here. I'm trusting God, Cal. Are you?"

She nodded. "Forever."

"Then go undercover for Shelby and Daniel, change your identity as many times as you need to while you're in the field. Because that's all a part of who you are. And I love that part just as much as all the others."

"Oh, Max, I love you so much." She threw herself into his arms and clung to him, then quickly let go, afraid she'd reopen his wound. "Sorry."

He grinned, kissed her. "Doesn't hurt a bit," he told her. "In fact, it feels really good."

They were leaving via the main door when Daniel and Shelby caught up to them.

"Oh, I forgot." Callie clapped a hand over her mouth. "I was supposed to go somewhere, wasn't I?"

"Home," Shelby said softly, her eyes brimming with tears. "You need to go home. You have three months of vacation time owing, Callie. I don't want to see you back at Finders until it's all used up."

"Thank you." She hugged her boss, then Daniel, too.

A few moments later Max whisked her away.

"Where are we going?"

"You'll see soon enough." He cradled her hand in his for a moment, then dropped it to change gears.

But she knew. She knew as soon as he started up the oak-lined street to the top of the hill.

Max pulled up in front of the house, shut off the engine and climbed out. He took Callie's hand and drew her to the front door.

"Welcome home, Mrs. Chambers," he whispered just before he lifted her in his arms and carried her over the threshold.

Home. It was such an awesome word. And this *was* home. It always had been.

She savored his embrace, returned his kiss with her own, whispered the words of love that had been pent up for far too long. And Max returned each. But in her private opinion Max drew away far too soon.

"There's just one more thing we have to do, Cal, before we make a brand-new start."

"There is?" She caught her breath when he drew the brown envelope from his jacket. She couldn't read the look in his eyes. They blazed with something that came from deep within. Regrets?

"I didn't look at them, Callie. I couldn't. You never wanted me to see them and I never will. Neither will anyone else. I think it's time we finally got rid of the past. Don't you?"

She nodded, followed him to the big circular fire pit they'd installed on the back patio for those chilly evenings when they wanted to watch the stars.

Without saying a word Max built a fire, adding fuel to it until it blazed and snapped spreading a glow of warmth across the bricks.

He drew a chair near the fire, pressed her into it, then stepped back.

"I'll be waiting inside, Cal. Whenever you're ready to start again."

He kissed her. Then his footsteps died away.

She was all alone.

Callie lifted the flap, drew out one of the pictures and stared at it. A face stared back at her, a face she barely recognized. The eyes brimmed with pain and shame and desperation—the eyes of a child who was hiding.

She tossed the photo onto the fire, watched a flame catch the corner, then greedily gobble up the rest. She pulled out a second picture. And after that, another.

Finally there was nothing left in the envelope and she tossed that onto the fire, too, watched as it burned, dissipated in a tiny pool of ash. The physical evidence was finally gone, but the past that lurked in the corners of her heart would take a little longer to disperse. She'd have to rely on God to get her through.

"I believe," she whispered as tears flowed down her cheeks. "I believe."

After a while gentle fingers curved over her shoulders, touching, soothing, loving.

"Don't regret what happened, Cal. That little girl of thirteen was very strong," Max whispered, drawing her up to stand in front of him.

His arms crossed her waist, snuggling her against him.

"She fought hard and long and she never gave up even though everyone let her down. I hope that one day we'll have a daughter as tough as she was."

Callie turned, stared into his eyes. "You mean it? You're not—*disgusted?*"

"By what they did to her, yes. But not by her. That girl, that precious child pushed her way through life. She learned how to take care of herself, to outwit the bad guys and to trust God to help her." His voice softened to a whisper. "That girl, Callie Merton, went undercover for a while, into a cocoon. But she emerged a beautiful woman who knows how to love and protect and care for those around her. That woman is the best wife any man could ask for. And I love her more today than I ever have."

He bent his head and kissed her.

"I love you, Max," she whispered, kissing him back.

He lifted his head. "Enough to go on a second honeymoon?"

Joy lifted Callie's heart in a song of praise and worship that God had done this—for her.

"Where?"

"I was thinking of camping—in the mountains," he teased.

"Wonderful." Then she stood on her tiptoes and showed him that it really didn't matter where they were.

Anywhere with God and Max was Heaven on earth.

* * * * *

Dear Reader,

Hello there! Welcome back to Finders, Inc.

Secrets are funny things, aren't they? Some are good—like Christmas secrets. And some can really drag you down, prevent you from living a full, rich life that shows the world your true colors. Callie's secret forced her to live in fear and shame for many years, until she realized that God had already forgiven her. But that forgiveness wasn't effective until she finally forgave herself.

I hope you'll trust the God who loves you with your secret. I pray you'll dig until you find His perfect peace, His joy unspeakable, His hope for you. Most of all, I pray you'll experience His love—beyond measure, beyond understanding, beyond description.

Blessings to you, friend.

Lois Richer

QUESTIONS FOR DISCUSSION

1. Everyone has secrets to hide. Think back over your life and discuss some unusual ones—your own or someone else's—and why you kept them a secret.

2. Max's reaction to sensing a change in Callie was to give her more space, to keep himself busier. While it's a common reaction, it often only exacerbates the underlying problem. Discuss why, and what Max might have done differently.

3. The nature of Callie's work meant she had to be self-reliant, even secretive. Share your thoughts on ways in which she could have formed a deeper connection to her husband and still protected the integrity of her job. Share whether you've ever used your job to exclude someone from your life.

4. Being alone is not the same as feeling lonely. Share an experience when you yourself felt lonely but were not alone. Where were you? Who were you with? How did you get through it?

5. Many times we recognize that something about a friend is not right, but we often hesitate to probe further lest we be accused of prying. Share ways of dealing with someone who is troubled and means of letting them know you care.

6. Callie struggled with loving Max and hurting him even more. She thought divorce was a way out of her dilemma. Discuss your views on the issues divorce resolves and/or creates for a husband and wife.

7. Callie made a lot of bad decisions, but near the end of the story she chose to leave Max rather than cause him more pain. Such desperate acts of valor aren't common in everyday life. Share your ideas of things we can do in our everyday lives to spare a neighbor, a friend, a parent, a child from pain or distress.

8. Hope lives in most of us even after we claim we've given up. Draw up a short list of things you're hoping to do, see or become. Choose one small step that you'll work toward in the coming weeks. Plan a party to celebrate, not only to mark an achievement, but also to recognize steps you're taking to get to your goal, or to help others achieve theirs.

REQUEST YOUR FREE BOOKS!

2 FREE INSPIRATIONAL NOVELS
PLUS 2
FREE
MYSTERY GIFTS

LoveInspired®

YES! Please send me 2 FREE Love Inspired® novels and my 2 FREE mystery gifts. After receiving them, if I don't wish to receive any more books, I can return the shipping statement marked "cancel." If I don't cancel, I will receive 4 brand-new novels every month and be billed just $3.99 per book in the U.S., or $4.74 per book in Canada, plus 25¢ shipping and handling per book and applicable taxes, if any*. That's a savings of at least 20% off the cover price! I understand that accepting the 2 free books and gifts places me under no obligation to buy anything. I can always return a shipment and cancel at any time. Even if I never buy another book from Steeple Hill, the two free books and gifts are mine to keep forever.

113 IDN EF26 313 IDN EF27

Name _____ (PLEASE PRINT) _____

Address _____ Apt. _____

City _____ State/Prov. _____ Zip/Postal Code _____

Signature (if under 18, a parent or guardian must sign)

Order online at www.LoveInspiredBooks.com

Or mail to Steeple Hill Reader Service™:

IN U.S.A.
P.O. Box 1867
Buffalo, NY
14240-1867

IN CANADA
P.O. Box 609
Fort Erie, Ontario
L2A 5X3

Not valid to current Love Inspired subscribers.

Want to try two free books from another series?
Call 1-800-873-8635 or visit www.morefreebooks.com

* Terms and prices subject to change without notice. NY residents add applicable sales tax. Canadian residents will be charged applicable provincial taxes and GST. This offer is limited to one order per household. All orders subject to approval. Credit or debit balances in a customer's account(s) may be offset by any other outstanding balance owed by or to the customer. Please allow 4 to 6 weeks for delivery.

LIREG06

Love Inspired® SUSPENSE

TITLES AVAILABLE NEXT MONTH

Don't miss these two stories in November

YULETIDE STALKER by Irene Brand

When a gorgeous woman walked off the plane in Hawaii, Linc Carey was stunned at the changes in Maddie Horton. She wasn't a gangly kid with braces anymore, and he definitely took notice. But with a stalker on their trail, would they live to see their blossoming love flourish?

MARRIED TO THE MOB by Ginny Aiken

The spitfire wife of recently slain mob boss was much more than FBI agent Dan Maddox had bargained for when he signed on to protect Carlotta Papparelli. Carlie was at the top of the mob's hit list, and they would stop at nothing to get to her.

LISCNM1006